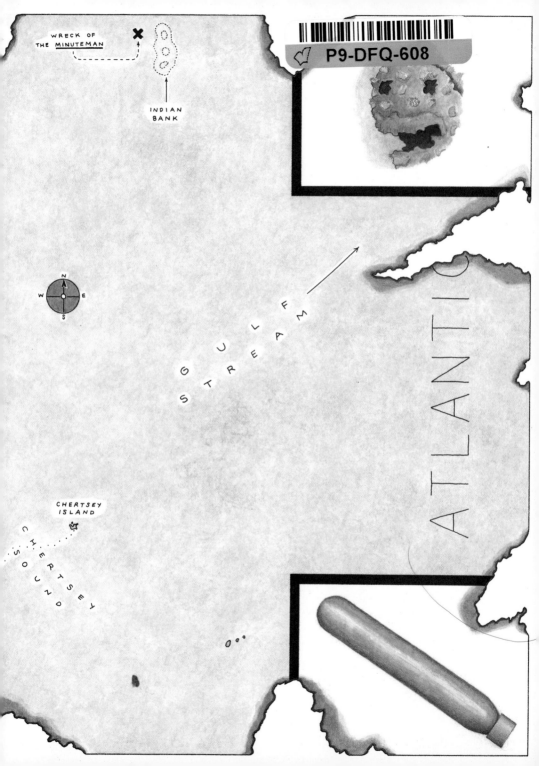

Chuck Dugan is AWOL

CHUCK DUGAN IS AWOL

A novel

With maps

ERIC CHASE ANDERSON

CHRONICLE BOOKS
SAN FRANCISCO

C

Library of Congress Cataloging-in-Publication Data:
Anderson, Eric Chase, 1973-

Chuck Dugan is AWOL : a novel with maps /
Eric Chase Anderson.

     p. cm.
ISBN 0-8118-3920-6
1.Absence without leave--Fiction. 2. Mothers
and sons--Fiction. 3.Treasure-trove--Fiction.
4. Remarriage--Fiction. 5. Midshipmen--Fiction.
6. Admirals--Fiction. I. Title.
PS3601.N543C47 2004
813'.6--dc21
                    2003009469

Text, illustrations, and design concept
by Eric Chase Anderson

Designed by Vivien Sung
Manufactured in Hong Kong

Distributed in Canada by Raincoast Books
9050 Shaughnessy Street
Vancouver, British Columbia V6P 6E5

10 9 8 7 6 5 4 3 2 1

Chronicle Books LLC
85 Second Street
San Francisco, California 94105

www.chroniclebooks.com

*** NOTE ***

Women were first admitted to the Naval
Academy in 1976, a fact that has been ignored for
the purposes of this book.

The Dugan Family Crest is based, with respect,
upon the Navy's "Master Diver" insignia.

Chuck quotes the Midshipman's Table of
Priorities from the guidebook <u>Reef</u> <u>Points</u>, published
by the Naval Institute Press of Annapolis, Maryland.

*** ACKNOWLEDGMENTS ***

The author is deeply indebted to Mr. P. Kent
Correll of New York City for his letters, stories,
photographs, and assistance.

Also, the author wishes to thank Lt. Grayson
Morgan, USN, for providing technical information and
encouragement.

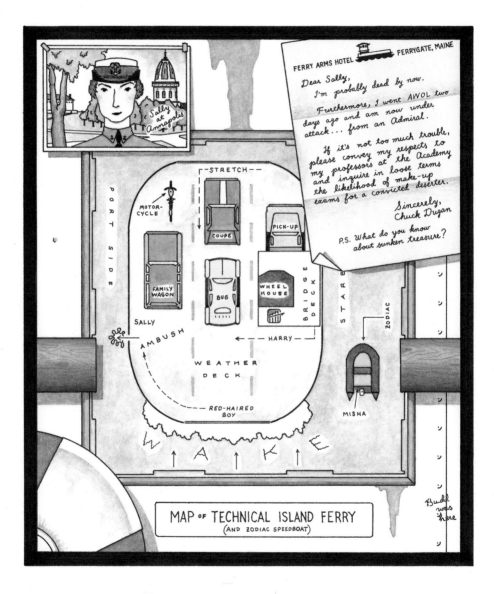

*** Chapter One ***

AMBUSH ON A FERRY

Ensign Sally Wisebadger, United States Navy,
was about to witness a drowning.

She was leaning against the ferry's metal rail,
letting the cold North Atlantic spray her fingertips.
She was in uniform: the crisply pressed tan trousers,
tan short-sleeve shirt, and collar pins of a single
gold stripe that signified her rank. She'd held that
rank, ensign, for under twenty-four hours. Yesterday,
she'd graduated from the Academy. This morning, she
was in the field.

The stumpy female-officer hat and bob of short
black hair framed her face -- it was a nice face --

frank, open, and thoughtful, with golden skin and a strong Apache nose. But the eyes were troubled.

Staring out at the still waters of Technical Bay, through which the ferry was passing, they failed to notice a haggard-looking figure moving toward her, up the port-side weather-deck. A hesitant, red-haired boy. Badly sunburnt. As he approached Sally in silence, weaving a trifle, he took up a position just behind her left ear -- and received a vicious blind punch in the neck. The blow came from nowhere, and sent him sprawling.

Waves crashing against the ferry's hull drowned out the sound. Sally heard nothing. The commotion went unnoticed by the nearby passengers.

And, for a moment, nothing else happened.

The boy had been preparing to speak to Sally, to form words in her ear. Did she know him? It was impossible to say. Was it to be a joke? A surprise? A secret? Who was he? She had not seen him and could not comment.

The boy was remarkable. Roughly eighteen, he was tall and lean, with an air of wildness. Here is a map of how he looked:

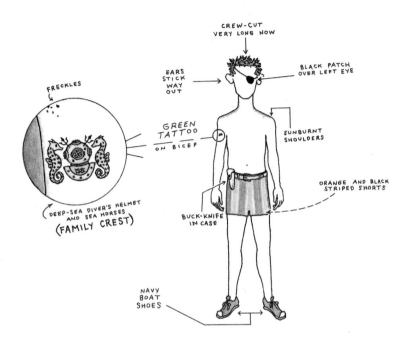

Now, he was flat on the deck.

Despite the obvious pain involved, the boy managed to struggle quickly onto his feet, blink away the tears, and square off with his attacker: a boy of darker hue, <u>gigantic</u> -- well over six feet -- and solid as a rock. A bit younger than his victim but of Polynesian extraction, the giant was dressed in almost-perfect monochrome: white shirt, black tie,

black trousers, green galoshes. He was trim, vast,
menacing.

The two boys faced each other in silence. Not
much of a place for a showdown.

The giant had the hoarse, scratchy throat of a
heavy teen smoker.

"Sorry, Little Dude," he croaked softly, balling
up one hand in the other like he was polishing his
fist. "Didn't mean to tag you so hard. Why don't you
just go back home, eh, Little Dude? Then we can put

a nice, rational end to all this open-hostilities
and mayhem crap."

The red-haired boy remained silent during this
speech. His hands, balled into fists, were held low,
at his hips. He said, "I _am_ home," and took three
steps backward.

Now Sally saw him. The boy met her gaze and
locked onto it. Her eyes widened perceptibly.

The moment was suspended in time.

Then a noise --

Shlik!

The sound of a switch-blade knife opening.

So, the boy thought, a glum smile flickering
across his face, I've walked into an ambush.

Behind him, another figure had appeared. Older
than the giant and wiry as a rail, but with the same
tensed posture of attack. The new man wore bell-
bottom jeans, a striped fisherman's sweater, and a
cloth cap pulled low enough to give the illusion of
shadows for eyes. He'd been waiting for the red-
haired boy. The switch-blade knife held loosely in
his thin left hand.

STRETCH REILLY
PICK-POCKET

BLACKPOOL, ENGLAND

AGE:
UNKNOWN
?

The boy cast a furtive glance at his shoulder, locating this new foe, then turned all the way around to face Sally.

They knew each other. That much was plain. He seemed about to speak her name aloud, and she his -- but his time was up. He brushed past her, planted one foot on the rail, and dove overboard.

The second man moved instantly to the side, leaned over, and cursed in a bright Cockney accent:

"Holy <u>cats</u>, Harry!" He whipped his cap off, revealing a bald head with strands of wispy blond hair and tiny, angry red eyes set deep in his skull. "There he goes again, that slippery little bastard!"

Sally looked down. There was no trace of the boy. He had disappeared. A drop of twenty feet.

The giant, joining his companion with a sigh, clubbed his massive fists down on the rail, making it vibrate dully. "Crap," he said calmly.

"You don't suppose," the Cockney began a moment later, then paused. He sounded amazed. "You don't suppose the little bugger's <u>dead</u>, do you?"

The giant leaned over the side to stare down at the water with huge, placid brown eyes. He took the number counter out of his shirt pocket and gave it a solitary click. "Probably, Dude," he said.

Somewhere, close by and getting closer, a Zodiac's outboard engine was growling on the open sea.

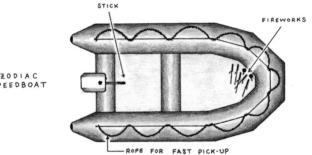

"Let's make a move," the Cockney urged, nudging his companion.

He turned away from the side and briefly faced Sally Wisebadger. As their eyes met, his conveyed the impression of words, of speech. All at once, Sally understood her peril. Whoever you are, the tiny red eyes seemed to say, I have seen you and will remember you. I am memorizing your face. You better forget you saw me because I will NOT be forgetting you. The switch-blade disappeared into his jeans pocket. With a slap at his bald head, the cloth cap extinguished the eyes.

The two attackers vanished into the crowd.

Less than a second passed. Sally's mind began to function. She whirled to the pilot house, cupped her hands to her mouth, and hollered:

"MAAN OVERBOARRD!"

Quickly, she found a life preserver ring, brought it up to the side like a discus, and scanned the water beyond the ferry -- you had to aim for the victim with one of these things; he might miss it, swim the other way. But she saw nothing, no-one. She raced aft, carrying the life preserver. Nothing behind. Nothing starboard either. People were beginning to collect around her. Attracted by the uniform. A bell started clanging. The deck heaved beneath their feet as the engines were thrown in reverse. <u>No-one</u> could hold their breath that long. There was no doubt about it.

The boy was dead.

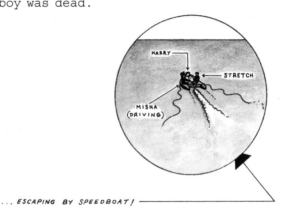

... *ESCAPING BY SPEEDBOAT!*

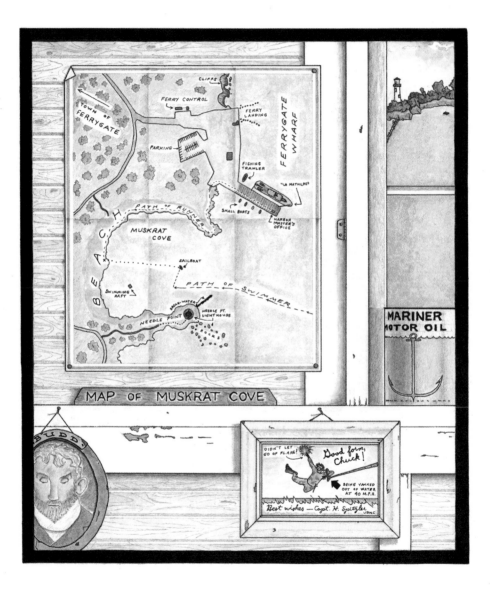

MAP OF MUSKRAT COVE

*** Chapter Two ***

CITIZEN'S ARREST

Exhaustion was nothing new to the boy.

(Not every college kid spent Spring Break with the Navy Frogmen.)

Nor was physical danger a novelty; he'd seen a lot the previous summer, training with the Marine Corps. He'd seen snakebite, fear, and a man shot in the knee.

He didn't dwell on it.

For the past hour, he had maintained a steady three and a half knots. He'd swum Technical Bay: four miles. A smooth, freestyle crawl -- his stroke of choice for long distances. His only worry when jumping

off the ferry had been the ferry's engines: done dif-
ferently, that move could have cost him a leg. However,
this boy knew something about boats. He knew, for
example, that the Technical Island Ferry's engines
were made in Holland by the Franco-Dutch firm of
Thiérry-Klüch and thus had a rather unique design:

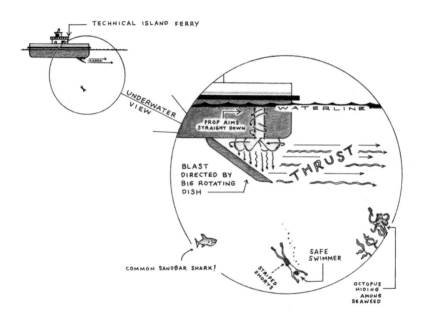

He had simply taken a giant breath and headed for
the bottom of the ocean, passing the big screw entirely.

To a less experienced diver, the idea would have
been crazy, terrifying. Even if Technical Bay was only

fifty feet deep, as it was. All that darkness. That vast, bone-chilling silence all around.

However, if he was nothing else, the boy was a natural swimmer. Part dolphin, some said. They said he could --

The boy slowed. He'd just heard something.

<u>There</u> <u>it</u> <u>was</u> <u>again</u>.

Two voices. They sounded young, like kids. Under water, where sound was muffled, the noises came shrill and faint. But unmistakable.

They were screams. Not playful ones. Coming from starboard. Perhaps forty feet to his right. Then, abruptly -- rrr-RRRRRRR! -- the big roar of an Evinrude ski-boat engine nearby. Accelerating hard.

A cold wave of fear shivered down the boy's spine.

Are they after me again? So soon?

The ski-boat raced past -- no more than a boat-length away -- and he dove instinctively beneath its wake. Then it sped out into the Bay. It left Muskrat Cove, which the boy had entered moments earlier, in its crazy, churning wake.

Either I'm under attack, the boy thought, letting the air in his lungs bring him gently upward, and this time on the open sea, or else some reckless idiot is hot-dogging in a much too powerful ski-boat.

Waves lapped over him as he bobbed to the surface. Treading water, he looked around to see what was happening.

He was right: a small sailboat had been capsized. Its slick, up-turned hull was visible, like a bright red turtle shell, sticking out of the water. Two kids, a little boy and an older girl, were clinging to the keel.

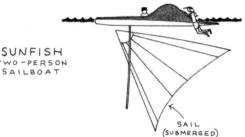

SUNFISH
TWO-PERSON
SAILBOAT

SAIL
(SUBMERGED)

He was furious. For him the ocean was not romper room -- it was not a playground. It was where he worked. It had rules.

"Help us!" the girl screamed. "We're slipping off!"

"YOU'RE SAFE," the boy called in a strong, steady voice. "I'M COMING."

He began swimming over.

"Stay calm and you'll be all right," he said to the girl. She looked down at him. Clinging by her fingernails, fear in her eyes, teeth chattering away.

"She's not a very good swimmer," the little boy called, from the other side of the boat.

"No," she corrected him, her voice shaky with fright. "I'm a _terrible_ swimmer. Who are you?" she asked.

"Name's Chuck Dugan." He sounded impossibly calm.

"I'm Eleanor. This is my brother, Danny."

"Nice to meet you, Eleanor; hiya, Danny."

"It's ... nice to meet _you_," the girl said. She seemed to be about thirteen. He held out his hand to shake. After a moment's hesitation, she reached out for it and slid off with a yelp! -- but he caught her and held her firmly to the side. They shook formally. She smiled.

"Pleased to meet you, mister," the boy called from his side of the boat, holding his hand out to shake. Chuck grinned; he liked the "mister." He ducked beneath the boat, brushing the mast -- aimed straight down -- and came up on the other side. The little boy was about ten. "You an islander, mister?" he asked as he shook Chuck's hand.

"Yep. From Chertsey."

The boy's eyes were wide.

"You're one of those Dugans?"

Chuck nodded. "One of them."

The boy gave an impressed whistle. "Boy! You guys are loaded!"

His sister shushed! him angrily, and Danny turned red.

Chuck shrugged. What could he say? No? We're not loaded? Anyway, what was the difference? He started to work on getting the boat turned upright again.

A disaster had been averted.

Over the minutes that followed, the boy and girl took Chuck's orders as he gave them -- feet on the keel, haul on that line, all together now: alley-OOP! -- saving not only their lives but their little sailboat as well. Chuck had righted many such small vessels in his years as a sailor.

Soon all three stood on the beach, surrounded by a crowd of on-lookers. Chuck had dragged the sailboat, undamaged, up into the shallows. Thanks and congratulations rained down on his sunburnt shoulders. A woman with an instant camera stepped forward, said, "Say

cheese, young man," and snapped a picture -- she
thought she might give it to the local newspaper.

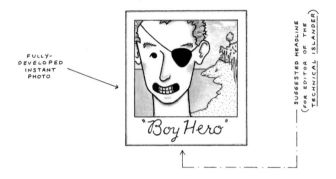

Chuck scarcely took notice.

"QUIET!" he commanded. His head was cocked,
listening intently.

A silence fell. It seemed odd in the sunlight
and heat.

One man, smoking a long-stemmed pipe he'd bought
in Germany several summers earlier, stopped patting
Chuck's back and turned to his wife. "Kind of a rude
kid, don't you think, baby?" he whispered. She didn't
answer. Everyone was listening.

First like a soft wind, then like a murmuring
voice, and now like a violin going thru - UUM! -- the

ski-boat rounded a corner of the dunes to the north and burst into Muskrat Cove, sending jets of water high into the air.

The crowd on the beach started yelling.

"What a nerve!" "Stop that jackass!" "Somebody call the cops! Call the Harbor Patrol!"

Clearly visible at the controls were a group of grinning young men: hell-raisers. A styrofoam cooler was thrown overboard. Laughter followed.

The man with the German pipe, planning to say, "Well, buddy, you seem to know what you're about after all," turned to make his apologies to Chuck Dugan --

But Chuck was long gone.

The Harbor Master's office, a small gray box at the end of the Ferrygate town pier, lay five hundred yards away. Chuck estimated he could cover the distance in under six minutes.

What a day! he thought as he ran along the beach. It's only ten o'clock in the morning, and already I've competed in the first two legs of an Olympic triathlon. What's next? The bike race?

The sand felt hot through the soles of his shoes.

He kept to the high-water line, where it was hard-packed and easier for running.

How did I get myself into this position? Chuck wondered. How did it all start? Then he remembered.

It was at Mail Call. Tuesday. Four days ago. He'd received a Letter, a Map, and an Invitation.

The Letter came from the family lawyer.

KERKWELL & SMITH ATTORNEYS **5TH AVENUE NEW YORK**

Dear Chuck,

When your father and I were captives together in the War, we made a solemn pact: to look after the other guy's family, should the worst come to pass. Since his untimely death in that godawful Observatory fire eight years ago, I've tried to hold up my end of the bargain.

Today, as you know, is your eighteenth birthday. Along with this heartfelt letter of congratulations, I am sending you a Treasure Map.

Budd called it "Chuck's Inheritance."

I don't know anything more about it. He entrusted it with me, and now, as instructed, I give it to you. Whether you go on this adventure -- whether you save it for a rainy day -- the choice is yours. My only advice is keep the damn thing secret.

As ever, you can contact me for help or further advice. Budd was my dearest friend, and our deal was for life.

Your affectionate uncle,
Gus Kerkwell

P.S. I was very alarmed to hear that your mother has become engaged to a man known as "The Admiral." At one time, your father planned to arrest this man for treason. You should contact her immediately. I could not get through. G.

Included with the Letter, Chuck found a Treasure Map -- torn, tattered, very old-looking. His father had made it.

Then he opened an envelope from home with the following inside:

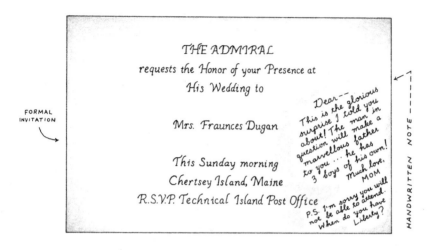

THE ADMIRAL
requests the Honor of your Presence at
His Wedding to

Mrs. Fraunces Dugan

This Sunday morning
Chertsey Island, Maine
R.S.V.P. Technical Island Post Office

Dear --
This is the glorious surprise I told you about! The man in question will make a marvellous father to you ... he has 3 boys of his own!
Much love,
MOM
P.S. I'm sorry you will not be able to attend. When do you have Liberty?

HANDWRITTEN NOTE -------

One helluva Mail Call! Chuck thought as he ran. Which had been harder to take in? The part about TREASURE? Or that bit about a WEDDING?

He just couldn't figure it. Why hadn't his mom told him? And who was this Admiral?

Chuck addressed a sandpiper as he ran past:

"He's a gold-digging scoundrel, that's who he is -- and so are his sons."

He ran up a flight of wooden steps -- from the beach to the wharf -- then turned right, starting down the long wooden dock toward the Harbor Master's office, his wet shoes squishing in rhythm, his mind drifting back to that evening, Tuesday night.

Chuck had drawn Guard Detail.

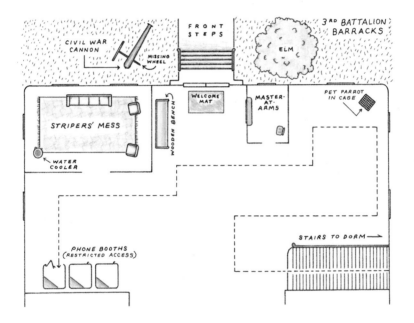

For ten full minutes on the hour -- every hour -- he stood at the pay phone until deep into the Middle Watch, trying to get through to his home in Maine.

No-one answered.

Finally, at three o'clock in the morning, a stranger picked up.

"Yeah!" the voice said.

"Mrs. Dugan, please."

"She's asleep. Who the hell is this?"

"Wake her up."

"Who wants her?"

"Her son."

A long pause.

"Hang on, Dude."

After a considerable wait -- the long-distance operator made him feed another five dimes into the phone -- a deep, slow voice came on the line.

"Good evening, this is the Admiral."

The picture of courtesy.

"This is Chuck Dugan, and I better get to talk to my mom right now!"

The Admiral calmly explained that, if Chuck interfered in any way, he would live to regret it -- IF HE LIVED AT ALL.

And I damn near didn't, Chuck thought as he ran, touching a finger to the eye patch covering his left eye. The eye beneath was badly burned: shot with a

Roman candle Wednesday morning as he stepped off the train at Hammersmith Depot. "The Boys" had turned out to be the Admiral's private army: his illegitimate sons, Stretch Reilly, Harry Aloha, and "the Lunatic." Name unknown. Chuck hadn't seen him yet.

Standing in Bancroft Hall Tuesday night, Chuck hung up the phone, removed his gun belt, walked up four flights, crawled out his dorm room window, and went Absent Without Leave.

Climbing down the drainpipe, dressed in black, he'd paused at the sound of his best friend Jim Burroughs, the Marine midshipman, singing softly in the darkness -- a song of cowboys and firelight and big Texan skies, the sorrowful melody floating out an open window ...

Enough already! Chuck thought, cutting the memories short. He kicked himself for letting his mind drift like that. Right now he needed to stay focused. Rapping sharply on the Harbor Master's door, Chuck turned the handle and entered at once.

"I'm here to make a Citizen's Arrest," were the first words out of his mouth.

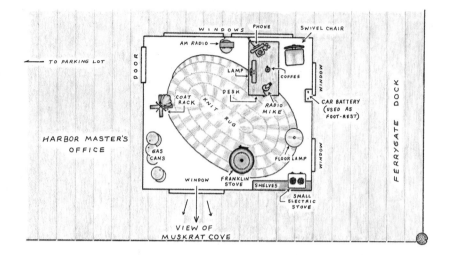

The blond-haired, blond-bearded Harbor Master, seated behind a small cluttered desk, newspaper in one hand, coffee in the other, looked up at his animated visitor. Before he had a chance to make any sort of response, Chuck crossed to the southwest-facing window and pressed a fingertip to the glass.

"Look," he commanded.

The man stood and joined Chuck at the little window that overlooked Muskrat Cove.

It was a provocative sight: the crowd of bathers gathered on the beach, staring and pointing angrily at the water; the hot-dogging ski-boat, banking and dancing crazily this way and that across the cove. Its occupants in hysterics, laughing and waving.

"They capsized a Sunfish. No injuries to report."

The Harbor Master's face turned purple. Few things were able to do that to him, since he was normally a patient and subdued man. But this was one of those things. Snatching up a radio on his desk, he called aloud to the Harbor Patrol, the division of the local police that oversaw boats and people on the water.

Chuck moved to the office door, opened it, and saw men already jogging down a gangplank to a police motor-boat. Its engines started, colored lights began to swirl, and it backed out of its berth. Within seconds the police were motoring quickly across the harbor, around the jetty, and into Muskrat Cove.

The Harbor Master, watching at the window, turned to face the boy.

He knew him, of course. Everyone around here did. It was Chuck Dugan.

With a puzzled frown on his face, he spoke:

"Afternoon, Chuck."

Literally shocked to hear his name, Chuck whipped around to face the Harbor Master. "I didn't recognize you there, Gary!" Chuck's eyes were watering. He looked away; then he sneezed. "Hayfever!" he declared, sneezing again.

The Harbor Master returned to his desk and passed a box of tissues across to Chuck. Chuck blew his nose honkingly.

"You were too busy," the Harbor Master said.

"I guess so!" HONK! Chuck gave it one last blow.

"Good work, by the way ..." the Harbor Master jerked his thumb in the direction of the cove. "You right that Sunfish all by yourself? Pretty tough to do single-handed."

Chuck glared at the floor; his gaze was steady. "Easy enough," he answered cautiously.

"What'd you do to your eye?"

Chuck looked up at him. "Huh? What do you mean?"

The Harbor Master smiled; he'd let that one pass. "Not in uniform, eh? On Liberty, I guess."

"Shore Leave, you mean."

"Right ... Are you?"

There was a long silence. A silence in which many

things in particular were not being said. Chuck's face
was blank, his hands hanging limp at his sides.

"Well, anyways ..." the Harbor Master finally
said. He waved at the radio-microphone on his desk.

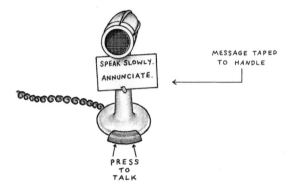

"I just got a report over the radio?" It was a
question -- of sorts -- and Chuck's head swiveled up to
the older man, who was peering into the boy's face.
Watching him like a hawk.

"It seems you jumped off the ferry a little while
ago, Chuck. You went overboard. _And_ ..." he said, eyes
wide, cocking his head at an amazed angle, "I can only
assume you swam the Bay just now. Christ knows how. You
want to tell me about any of that?"

"Not especially."

"You don't want to explain?"

"No, sir."

"Well, it was a _very_ dangerous thing to do, pal."

"Yeah?"

"Not to mention the fact that there's a whole lot of people who think you're _dead_ right now. Including your mother, for one!"

For a long, unsteady moment, Chuck seemed to consider what the man had said. Maybe -- well, what the hell. Maybe he _did_ want to talk about it. Maybe it was best to call this thing off. Bring in re-enforcements. After all, what would his old pal Jim Burroughs think about what he was doing? Jim would grin and say, You're out-manned, Chuck. Out-gunned and outta time. Your hand is to FOLD, amigo. Plain and simple.

Chuck gave a weary sigh. He seemed to slump: exhausted, defeated. Water dripped from his nose to a puddle on the floor.

Then Gary, the Harbor Master, picked up the microphone, flipped on the radio, and began to speak:

"Ferry Control. Ferry Control. This is Harbor Master. -- Have got missing ferry passenger in my office. Identified as Dugan, Charles, of Chertsey I. That's D - U - G ----!"

Chuck snatched away the mike, hurled it through the window, and ran -- ran? he <u>sprinted</u> -- out the door and down the dock to his beat-up Ford Ranch Wagon, parked in the visitors lot. The whole reason he'd swum here in the first place: his disguise kit was inside.

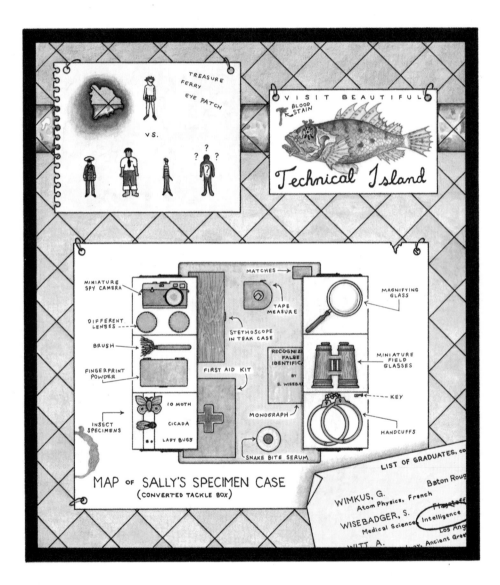

*** Chapter Three ***

EVIDENCE

Sally crouched on the deck of the ferry, looking through her magnifying glass.

"Hmmmm," she murmured and closed an eye.

She'd found a thumb-print.

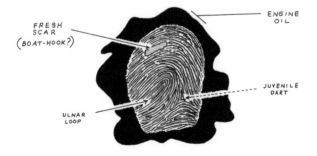

Was it Chuck's?

She would check her files.

She moved on, across the deck. It was warmer here than in the Bay. They were docked at Technical Island -- they had been for forty-five minutes. Seagulls wheeled overhead. Sally turned, watching them go. Large New England <u>Larus</u> <u>argentatus</u>. Common. But interesting.

Her gaze moved farther out: to the <u>Kestrel</u> -- a U.S. Navy patrol vessel anchored in the Bay. Sleek. War-like. Its presence made Sally uneasy. What was it doing here? She had no idea.

She knelt and removed a tape measure from her case.

There was a footprint here. Several, in fact. One stood out.

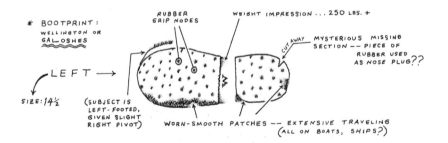

* BOOTPRINT :
WELLINGTON OR
GALOSHES

RUBBER
GRIP NODES

WEIGHT IMPRESSION ... 250 LBS. +

CUT AWAY MYSTERIOUS MISSING
SECTION -- PIECE OF
RUBBER USED
AS NOSE PLUG??

LEFT →

SIZE: 14½

(SUBJECT IS
LEFT-FOOTED,
GIVEN SLIGHT
RIGHT PIVOT)

WORN-SMOOTH PATCHES -- EXTENSIVE TRAVELING
(ALL ON BOATS, SHIPS?)

A shadow fell across the deck. Sally looked up.

"Planning on doing some fishing while you're here, ma'am?" The Chief of Police was watching her work.

"I beg your pardon?"

He pointed at the case beside her. "It's a tackle box, isn't it?" He frowned. "_Isn't_ it?"

Sally glanced at her Specimen Case. "Oh -- yes, I suppose it is," she said, closing it quickly. "What can I do for you, Chief?"

"Nothing. Just wanted to see if you were all right."

"Fine, thanks."

"Let me know if you need anything, OK?"

"There is one thing."

"Shoot."

"I need to visit the bridge."

"What for?"

"Information."

He frowned. "Go on up there when you're ready ... Say -- you're not a _spy_ or something, are you, ma'am?"

Sally didn't seem to hear him. She picked up her case and moved toward the rail where Chuck had jumped overboard an hour earlier.

Wedged against a steel bolt holding this section of deck in place -- was a firecracker.

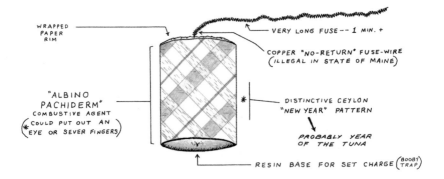

"Hmm," Sally said, turning it in her hand. "Troubling."

Did it belong to Chuck? Had he picked it up in the South Seas? Diving that wrecked battleship off the Solomons last Christmas?

Sally straightened. She'd searched the deck. It was time to examine the bridge.

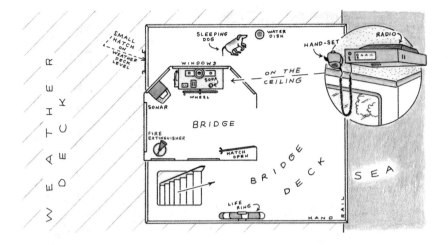

It was empty. No clues. Through the windows she
could see activity outside:

Police were interviewing the last of the
passengers on-deck. Boats were visible near the site
of the accident.

Searching, Sally thought grimly, for Chuck.

Her fingers thrummed the wheel, then gripped
it tight. He isn't dead, she thought. Not till I've
examined the body myself. And know the exact cause
of death.

She was disappointed with her evidence. It was
all circumstantial. Chuck had been waiting for her --
that was her theory. The bridge was the last place
she'd checked. And there was no sign of him.

Something on-deck caught Sally's eye.

"You OK, ma'am?" The Chief stood in the open
hatchway. He had followed her.

"I have a question for you," she said.

"Shoot."

She reached into her case and removed the pair
of field glasses. With her free hand she pointed
through the window. "Who is that man?"

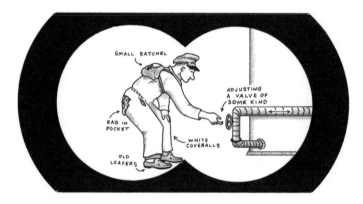

The Chief nodded. "That's E.R."

"E.R.?"

"Right -- we let him off to get supplies. There's
quite a line building up on the other side of the
Bay, as you might imagine. They're plenty anxious to
get underway."

"They? Who's they?"

"Ferry Control."

"Is he the captain of this ferry?"

"No, he's the engineer."

She could have kicked herself. "Who else works belowdecks?"

"Nobody. Just him."

Sally watched the engineer. One detail stuck out.

Her heart skipped a beat. She'd seen that symbol before --

Just then, a voice crackled on the cabin radio. Sally brought her binoculars down. The Chief turned to hear it.

Clearly, but through heavy static, the voice said:

"FERRY CONTROL. FERRY CONTROL. THIS IS HARBOR

MASTER. HAVE GOT MISSING FERRY PASSENGER IN MY OFFICE.
IDENTIFIED AS DUGAN, CHARLES, OF CHERTSEY EYE. THAT'S
DEE. YOU. GEE. --!"

It cut itself off.

Sally's and the Chief's eyes met.

The Chief snatched the hand-set from its cradle
and spoke into it urgently. "Harbor Master! Harbor
Master! Say again! Lost your message! Please say
again! ... Harbor Master, do you read me?"

He clicked the TALK button several times. Then
he pointed at one of his deputies. "See that man,
miss?"

"Yes, Chief."

"<u>Would</u> <u>you</u> <u>send</u> <u>him</u> <u>up</u> <u>here</u> <u>immediately</u>?"

He spoke into the radio again. "Harbor Master,
this is Technical Island Police sending. Can you
read me?"

Sally left the bridge with the Chief's voice
ringing in her ears. The deputy took one look at the
expression on her face and dashed up the companionway.
Sally stood alone on the deck, silent and perfectly
still.

What was going on?

What was Chuck up to?

What did that engineer know about it?

"The backpack," she whispered. "Chuck's backpack." Her eyes narrowed. That was one thing she could find out about on her own.

Turning, she faced an innocent-looking hatch in the white super-structure. The engineer had disappeared through it moments earlier. She gave each of the water-tight handles a twist and swung the hatch open. Slowly, cautiously, she entered. The hatch creaked shut behind her.

Sally stood inside a dim chamber the size of a telephone booth. Her eyes took a moment to adjust. A ladder led straight through the floor.

Its iron rungs echoed as she climbed down. _Tink ... tink ... tink ..._

A deep vibration now as the engines powered to life. The rumble and crash made Sally's teeth chatter. She grabbed the ladder and held on. After a moment, it grew quieter.

She took a deep breath. Then a step.

Tink ... TINK!

She had reached the bottom.

A flashlight dazzled her eyes.

"Can I help you?" a deep voice boomed.

Sally jumped. She held up a hand to shade her face.

"Ensign Wisebadger," she said. "U.S. Navy."
She flashed her ID. "I'd like to ask you a few
questions, sir."

"I've got a ferry to run."

"It's about Chuck Dugan."

The flashlight snapped off. "Let's make this
quick."

"OK."

"Don't touch anything."

"I can't even _see_."

"Take my hand."

He led the way.

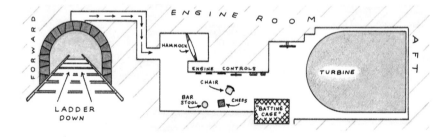

"You a pal of Chuck's?" the engineer asked.
They were moving down a dark and narrow corridor.

"I was his Company Commander."

"At Annapolis?"

"Yessir."

"You must feel right at home here."

"I studied medicine, actually."

"Then _really_ don't touch anything."

He led her past a wall of dials and meters, and gestured to a steel chair for her to sit. The noise from the big turbine was loud. Though not, Sally noticed thankfully as she sat, as loud as it had been in the stairwell.

"Cup of coffee?"

"Please."

He moved to an area that looked like a tiny batting cage: fenced in on all sides, it featured a hot plate, shelves, and hooks for jackets. He stooped under thick pipes to enter it. Sally noticed Chuck's backpack hanging from a strap.

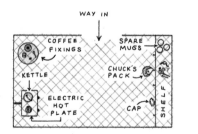

- 47 -

"What's 'E.R.' stand for?" she asked.

He looked at her in surprise. "ENGINE ROOM!"

She couldn't help laughing. "Unusual name for a person."

"You think so? Archibald McChesney, then." He brought out two mugs of instant coffee. "Now what can I do for the Navy that the Navy can't do for itself?"

"Did you see Chuck this morning?"

"Sure."

"Have you told the police?"

"Why should I?"

A new thought occurred to her. "Mister McChesney --" she began.

"E.R."

"-- Are you aware that we've been stopped here for the past hour?"

"Of course. I stopped us."

"Do you know why we stopped?"

"Oh -- some damn silliness or other."

"Chuck Dugan jumped overboard in the middle of the Bay."

He frowned. He sipped his coffee. "Technical Bay?"

"Yessir."

"Jumped <u>overboard</u>?"

"Yessir."

He whistled. He shook his head. He blew on his coffee and began taking gulps of it. His face was red.

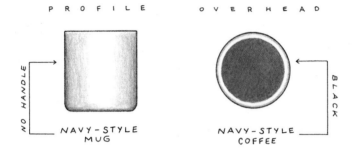

"Is Chuck dead?" he asked.

"We thought he was," Sally answered slowly. "But it looks like he may have swum back."

"Swum back ... to <u>Maine</u>?"

"Yessir. Can I ask a question?"

"OK."

"Why are you carrying his backpack around?"

He shrugged. "For supplies."

"Was Chuck here?"

"Since five o'clock this morning."

"Doing what?"

"Drinking coffee. Playing chess."

"He left at some point?"

"Every time we pulled in to Ferrygate. Went up, took a look, came back down -- until this last trip. Then he stayed topside. What about you?"

She was taking notes. She looked up. "Beg pardon?"

"You eating lunch down here or what?"

Sally smiled. "No -- thanks very much."

"I got kielbasa sauerkraut."

"No --"

"Mrs. E.R. fixed it."

"No, thank you. I have to go. Just one more --"

"Question? OK, but _Christ_ you Navy kids are nosy."

"Did Chuck leave anything behind?"

He looked at her like she'd gone crazy. "What have we been _talking_ about?"

Sally said: "His backpack."

She went into the batting cage and lifted Chuck's bag off the hook.

"It's empty," she said.

"I took out all the crap. Saved it. He's a friend of mine. Gave my engines a tune-up last week. Can you believe it? A kid that age? Eighteen years old, he's got my engines running like a Swiss watch."

"Where are his things?"

"Look up!"

On the shelf above, Sally found this collection of objects:

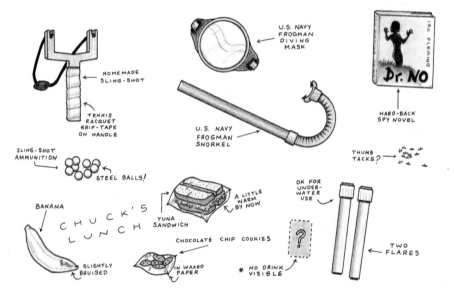

HOMEMADE
SLING-SHOT

TENNIS
RACQUET
GRIP-TAPE
ON HANDLE

U.S. NAVY
FROGMAN
DIVING
MASK

HARD-BACK
SPY NOVEL

SLING-SHOT
AMMUNITION

STEEL BALLS!

U.S. NAVY
FROGMAN
SNORKEL

THUMB
TACKS?

CHUCK'S LUNCH

BANANA

SLIGHTLY
BRUISED

TUNA
SANDWICH

A LITTLE
WARM
BY NOW

CHOCOLATE CHIP COOKIES

IN WAXED
PAPER

OK FOR
UNDER-
WATER
USE

* NO DRINK
VISIBLE

TWO
FLARES

After examining them, she discovered two printed items, lying underneath.

This:

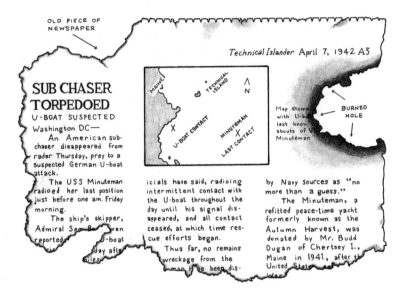

OLD PIECE OF NEWSPAPER

Technical Islander April 7, 1942 A3

SUB CHASER TORPEDOED

U-BOAT SUSPECTED

Washington DC—

An American sub-chaser disappeared from radar Thursday, prey to a suspected German U-boat attack.

The USS Minuteman radioed her last position just before one am. Friday morning.

The ship's skipper, Admiral Sam Bo___wen reported ___ U-boat ___ day aft___ ___iles ___

Map shows ___ with U-b___ last know ___ abouts of U___ Minuteman

BURNED HOLE

MAINE

TECHNICAL ISLAND

N

U-BOAT CONTACT
X

MINUTEMAN
X
LAST CONTACT

icials have said, radioing intermittent contact with the U-boat throughout the day until his signal disappeared, and all contact ceased, at which time rescue efforts began.

Thus far, no remains wreckage from the ___ have been dis-

by Navy sources as "no more than a guess."

The Minuteman, a refitted peace-time yacht formerly known as the Autumn Harvest, was donated by Mr. Budd Dugan of Chertsey I., Maine in 1941, after th___ United Stat___ ___

And this:

FORMAL INVITATION CARD

The Admiral requests
the pleasure of your company
at a Rehearsal Dinner and Reception

The Dugan Family Home
Chertsey Island, Maine

RIP

COFFEE STAIN

Saturday Night
Eight o'clock
R.S.V.P. Technical Island Post Office

After a minute, E.R. came over and saw the invitation in Sally's hands.

"Yeah," he said, nodding. "Chuck said something about a party tonight ... What are you grinning at?"

"Nothing," Sally said.

She had evidence -- hard evidence -- and the beginnings of a plan.

*** Chapter Four ***

ROOM SERVICE

FERRY ARMS HOTEL   FERRYGATE, MAINE

GUEST REGISTER

NAME *Rudolph Bradshawe* HOMETOWN *P'burgh*

CHILDREN *Junior* PETS *Nada* SPECIAL NEEDS *24-HOUR ROOM SERVICE!*

CHECK-OUT DATE *Will Advise...*

"Good afternoon, Mr. Bradshawe," the front desk clerk said cheerfully. Part of his job at the Ferry Arms Hotel was to have the guests' names memorized from the day they arrived. The Bradshawes, father and son, had been at the hotel for the better part of a week now. No check-out date. "And how are we today?"

The gruff, middle-aged figure gave an impatient wave of the hand. His eyes were invisible behind dark glasses. In the other hand he held the curved bamboo handle of an umbrella.

The desk clerk wondered why. That is, why the man carried that umbrella around with him all the time -- it hadn't rained, not for three weeks. But Mr. Bradshawe -- Rudolph Bradshawe, from Pittsburgh, Pennsylvania -- was an odd man. A bit of Mark Twain, the desk clerk mused, considering the man's nineteenth-century appearance: sideburns, whiskers, shaggy gray eyebrows.

"Front!" Mr. Bradshawe shouted, looking around. He slapped the silver counter-bell repeatedly.

With a dash of Genghis Khan, the desk clerk concluded, thinking of the man's manners. The clerk gave a patient smile. "I can help you myself, sir. What is it that you require?"

"Expecting a package, young man!" Shouting.

Mr. Bradshawe was always shouting.

"... Y-es. I have a note from Mr. Bradshawe, Junior, to that effect." The clerk held up an index card and read aloud: "Skin-diving gear." He looked up. "Anything else?"

Mr. Bradshawe whirled away. "Roger! Send up a tuna-fish sandwich and a cold glass of milk! And I mean cold!" He hollered this over his shoulder, bustling across the lobby. It was a handsome country inn with lots of nautical touches: brass rails here and there and a brass dinner bell, mahogany floors, regatta trophies in a trophy case, and a sleeping cat in the corner. Mr. Bradshawe, a big man who liked to move fast, headed straight up the staircase.

"Right away, sir," the desk clerk called after him. "Oh, and -- sir? Any chocolate chip cookies to go with that?"

"What do YOU think?" the voice bellowed from the second-floor landing.

The desk clerk nodded his head and took down the order with a pencil. The Bradshawes liked their chocolate chip cookies.

The key turned in the lock, and Mr. Bradshawe entered his hotel room. He shut the door tightly behind him. Turning back, he scanned the room with a cool, appraising eye. What could he be looking for? There was nothing, really, to see.

The bed had been made, of course, like any hotel. And, like any good hotel, there were fresh towels in the bath, fresh fruit in the bowl, and a small mint on his pillow.

Mr. Bradshawe behaved as if the room were not really his. He made no sound of any kind. Kneeling, he looked under the bed. He stood and blew his hands clean of dust. He crossed quietly to the window, staying on the rug and off the polished hardwood floor, and gazed down onto the back lawn of the Ferry Arms Hotel.

Shady with tall birch, maple, and pine trees, the grass sloped down past white deck chairs and a tennis court to a small private beach. A few sailboats were moored at the end of a short dock.

Mr. Bradshawe faced the room. He needed to get some shut-eye if he could.

Sally ... Her face flashed through his mind.

Standing in profile on the ferry, the wind in her hair. This very morning, he thought to himself wistfully. Seems like a week ago!

It had come as no great surprise, her being on that ferry; he'd been expecting her for days. I've got to speak to Sally -- that's what he'd been telling himself all last week. He wondered what Sally had made of the two thugs he tangled with. Stretch and Harry. Would she believe they were brothers? No: she would laugh. So literal. So scientific. Boy, he thought, suddenly worried, I hope she didn't have any trouble with them. He wished he could talk to her about the two of them -- about them and many other things. More than anything in the world, practically, he wanted to discuss with her what was happening.

First things first ... He focused on the current situation.

Had anyone else been inside his room? It was difficult for him to tell. Probably not, he concluded -- aside from the maid.

This is what his room was like:

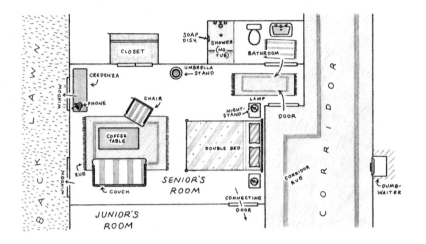

As a rule, he stayed out of the adjoining room
of the suite. That was Bradshawe, Jr.'s. And unless
he happened to <u>be</u> Bradshawe, Jr., he kept himself
confined to this room.

Bradshawe Junior <u>and</u> Bradshawe Senior?

It was confusing as hell, but that was part of
the plan. More faces to hide behind. The hotel staff
weren't curious; and he made sure -- with all that
curmudgeonly bluster -- that nobody really <u>wanted</u> to
talk to Bradshawe, Sr.

And if anybody ever got around to asking why it
was the two Bradshawes never seemed to be together in

the same place, he could always say Junior was off at camp or Senior was away on business. Whatever seemed good at the time.

The knock at the door gave him a start. Take it easy, he told himself. For crying out loud, it's just room service. Take ... it ... easy.

"Enter!" he hollered, after checking himself in the mirror that hung over the dressing table and unlocking the door. He snapped open a briefcase that lay on the credenza and yanked a sheaf of brochures from inside. This he did rather clumsily. The papers spilled onto the floor. "Christ!" he groaned.

The door opened, and a uniformed waiter came into the room carrying a silver tray with his lunch. What he always had: tuna fish and potato chips with milk and chocolate chip cookies to follow, beside a single yellow rose in a crystal one-stem vase.

Mr. Bradshawe, irritable, was on his knees monkeying with the mess of loose papers and swearing angrily under his breath.

"On the table, on the table," he said impatiently. "Leave yourself fifteen percent. _Just_ fifteen, mind you."

"Yes, sir," the waiter said, hurrying.

Bradshawe stood up to sign the check. As he rose, his gaze lingered for a moment on the waiter's feet, though he couldn't really say why.

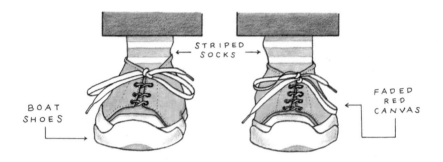

The feet were wearing boat shoes. So what? He wore boat shoes himself. This was a sea-side community. The guy probably owned a boat. Maybe one of the ones down at the hotel dock. He looked up, at the waiter's face -- he didn't mean to. Avoid eye contact, he'd been telling himself all week. But it was automatic. He glanced up at the waiter's face, and his eyes met the waiter's eyes.

This was a new one. This waiter. Bradshawe knew most of the staff by sight; he had a stolen copy of their work schedule in his briefcase, so he knew who worked and when.

The waiter was young, in his twenties, with a head of bushy black hair. It was the damnedest head of hair Bradshawe could ever remember seeing on a person who was indoors. It was hurricane hair. The young man's nose was long, his cheekbones high, and his eyes gray and intense.

The first of Bradshawe's silent alarms went off.

Oh, yes. This was a new one. He'd never seen him before in his life. As a matter of <u>fact</u> --

The silver tray was swinging at him through the air.

Bradshawe got his hand up in time.

CLANG! The tray bounced back, ringing like a bell.

The waiter scowled at his tray. It had hit the bamboo umbrella handle, but felt like it had struck metal.

<u>Under</u> <u>attack</u> <u>again</u>! Bradshawe sprang forward and kicked at the waiter's leg, trying to upset his balance and send him to the rug. His shoes were not very effective; they were rubber, too soft.

His kicks popped off bone, and the waiter
winced in pain but managed to bring the serving
tray back around the other way and connect with
Bradshawe's shoulder. WHUMP! Bradshawe stumbled; his
glasses flew to the floor. The two sprang away from
each other.

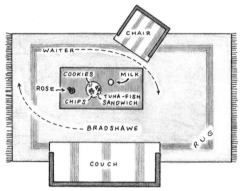

FIGHT
MAP

Circling, circling, studying each other's
defenses. The waiter had trained at a variety of hand-
to-hand combat techniques, it was obvious. Neither of
them seemed rushed or rattled.

"Take off that wig," the waiter said. It came
out sounding like <u>Tyek</u> <u>uff</u> <u>thet</u> <u>veek</u>.

Bradshawe straightened, surprised. Not at the
words but at the sudden accent. He narrowed his eyes.
"Which one are you?" he asked. His voice had changed,

too. A bit higher and clearer than before. Starting to sound more like a teenager.

"Why should I tell you anything?" sounded like <u>Vy shood aye tyell YOU any sink</u>?

"Why not? You afraid of me?"

Silence.

Bradshawe switched the umbrella to his other hand, gave the shaft a twist,

STEEL BLADE

and drew a thin sword out by the bamboo handle.

The waiter smiled in spite of himself. So <u>that's</u> what it was. "I like your umbrella."

"Keeps me dry."

"I am Misha --"

Bradshawe nodded. "His Russian son. Yeah, I've heard about you."

"Good things?" the Russian asked.

"No. Same things as the other two."

The Russian's face darkened into a scowl. "Which means what?"

"That you're a mad, ruthless bastard. Emphasis on the <u>bastard</u>."

The Russian grinned malevolently. "You know," he said quietly, "I'm glad we aren't just playing around anymore. I'm pleased at the recent escalation of hostilities between our two sides. It would be a shame not to get to kill you in actual fact."

"You'll find that harder than you think, comrade."

"Don't call me that," the Russian said. "I am not a communist. I was never a communist. I am a capitalist. Same as yourself -- yes?"

Bradshawe shrugged. "I'm just a sailor."

He saw his best opening yet: the Russian was in a narrow spot between the couch and the coffee table. Bradshawe made a sudden move like he was going to swing his sword -- then reached down and picked up the glass of milk instead. The Russian reacted by backing up to try and give himself room, but couldn't. He stumbled. Bradshawe, waiting for this, pegged the glass in a hard, direct line just as the Russian's head was exposed. It cracked him on the skull and, by some miracle, didn't shatter. At the last second, the Russian flung the silver tray in Bradshawe's direction. The tray made contact with the very top of Bradshawe's head, and for an instant seemed to have had the effect of scalping the man.

Milk went everywhere.

Bradshawe's hair lay on the floor: a wig.

The Russian gave a cry and collapsed, half on and half off the couch, drenched in ice-cold milk.

Chuck Dugan, wearing a gray three-piece suit and artificial sideburns, now lacking the gray wig, put his hand to his temple. It came away bloody.

"They found me," he muttered through clenched teeth as he lurched into the bathroom.

The telephone rang in the next room.

A wet towel pressed to his head, Chuck opened the connecting door, went in, and answered "Junior's" phone:

"Bradshawe!"

He listened for a moment.

"My son will be back momentarily! Thank you!"
He hung up.

He went back to his room and re-entered the
bathroom.

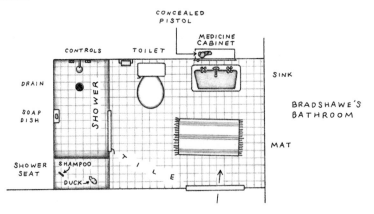

He bandaged his head as quickly as he could. To
the mirror he said: "You left your disguise kit in the
car, you nitwit. Well!" he gave a sigh. He was by
nature a very positive person. "I've always wanted to
try that dumbwaiter."

He opened the medicine cabinet, removed the
bundle of chamois concealing his pistol, and stuck
that under his arm.

Chuck took one last glance around his hotel room
-- knowing this was good-bye, his cover was blown, he
was homeless again. He also knew that Bradshawe, Jr.,
was expected at the front desk. It would not do for
Bradshawe, Sr., wearing a bloody wig and a torn coat,
to come bumbling downstairs. Plus, he didn't know
what his odds were for survival. Could be _anybody_
waiting in the lobby. The big Hawaiian. The skinny
Englishman. Could be the _Admiral_ _himself_.

This was part of his whole problem, Chuck
realized: he needed better intelligence. Without
glancing at the prostrate Russian on his couch, he
searched the fallen young man's pockets and came
up with an engraved, cream-colored invitation card.
It looked familiar to him. He slid it inside his
vest. Then he picked up sandwich, cookies, wig,
stuffed them all in his jacket pockets, and left
the room, hanging the DO NOT DISTURB sign on the
doorknob.

In the wall of the corridor directly opposite
his and Junior's suite was a panel, halfway up from
floor to ceiling.

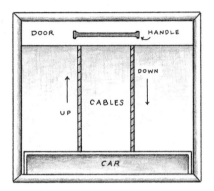

The dumbwaiter's function was to bring meals from the kitchen to the rooms upstairs and back down again. It was not meant for people.

Chuck looked down the hall; then he squeezed himself inside the dumbwaiter. It was not the least bit claustrophobic; once, Chuck spent two whole weeks in a nuclear missile submarine at the bottom of the sea. This was nothing to that.

He slid the panel shut behind him.

Cre-_eak_! ... Cre-_eak_! ...

The muffled sound that followed was Chuck lowering himself, inch by inch, down to the basement.

Twenty minutes later, young Rudy Bradshawe, looking like he'd just arrived from a pleasant morning's lifeguard duty at the beach, appeared at the front desk and signed for a delivery of skin-diving equipment. The cases all read Hammersmith Oceanographic Institute on the sides. He needed help getting them loaded into the back of his station wagon, and he tipped the porters handsomely. Everyone who worked at the Ferry Arms Hotel liked Bradshawe, Jr., and they wondered how he could put up with such a loudmouth for a father.

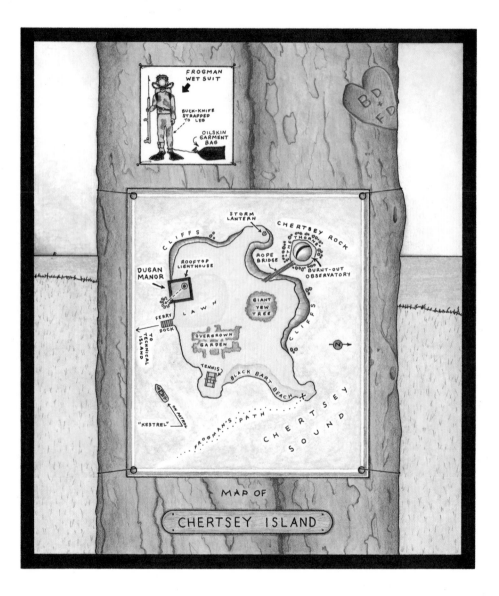

FROGMAN WET SUIT

BUCK-KNIFE STRAPPED TO LEG

OILSKIN GARMENT BAG

B D + F D

STORM LANTERN

CHERTSEY ROCK

CLIFFS

ROPE BRIDGE

THE THORNS

BURNT-OUT OBSERVATORY

DUGAN MANOR

ROOFTOP LIGHTHOUSE

GIANT YEW TREE

FERRY DOCK

LAWN

CLIFFS

TO TECHNICAL ISLAND

OVERGROWN GARDEN

N

TENNIS

BLACK BART BEACH

FROGMAN'S PATH

C H E R T S E Y   S O U N D

"KESTREL"
ON PATROL

MAP OF

CHERTSEY ISLAND

*** Chapter Five ***

THE PARTY

Bearing a silver tray with a single cut-glass tumbler on it, an elderly waiter shuffled through the crowd gathered in the warm evening air on Chertsey Island.

In the exact center of each of the many small tables he passed -- set up on the lawn by a professional catering company -- rested the large portrait of a man.

VIEW OF CHERTSEY →

Welcome to our Home

←----- STERLING FRAME

The waiter had passed the face many times without betraying any response to it.

He deposited his one-drink payload at the table of a solitary figure whose features were obscured by the brim of an extremely wide hat.

"Thank you, Brace."

"Not at all, sir."

The waiter turned away, then turned back. He leaned down and peered under the hat. Even at close range, it took him a moment.

"Master Charles?" he whispered. "Is that you?"

"I'm here to see my mother," Chuck replied.

He took a sip. He'd ordered his usual.

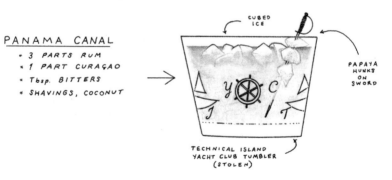

PANAMA CANAL
* 3 PARTS RUM
* 1 PART CURAÇAO
* Tbsp. BITTERS
* SHAVINGS, COCONUT

CUBED ICE

PAPAYA HUNKS ON SWORD

TECHNICAL ISLAND YACHT CLUB TUMBLER (STOLEN)

The old man watched him. His name was Brace. He had been the family butler for decades.

"May I ask what you did to your eye, sir?"

"Somebody shot it."

"Good heavens, sir. Shall I send for a doctor?"

"No thanks." Chuck lowered his voice. "How's Mom?"

The butler moved closer and spoke from behind his hand. "Being guarded round the clock, sir."

Chuck nodded. "That's what I figured." He pointed at the picture on his table. "She really gonna <u>marry</u> this guy?"

"Yes, sir. The wedding takes place tomorrow morning. Ten o'clock sharp."

"I gotta talk to her."

"Yes, sir. I'll see what I can do." The butler paused. "How is school, Master Charles?"

"I'm AWOL."

"Sorry to hear it, sir."

"You and me both," Chuck said, reaching inside his tunic pocket and bringing out a small wooden pipe.

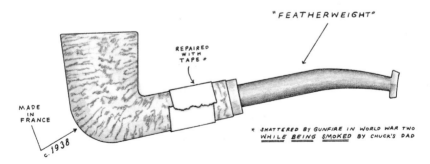

"FEATHERWEIGHT"

REPAIRED
WITH
TAPE *

MADE
IN
FRANCE

c. 1938

* SHATTERED BY GUNFIRE IN WORLD WAR TWO
WHILE <u>BEING</u> <u>SMOKED</u> BY CHUCK'S DAD

He stuck the pipe between his teeth and found a black lighter, which he flicked alight. He held the flame sideways to the pipe bowl, puffing vigorously to get the ember started as smoke billowed into a pleasant blue cloud around his head and he began coughing steadily.

The entire process he performed with his left hand only.

"AHOY, MARINE," boomed a deep voice.

Chuck lifted his head and squinted through the fog of tobacco.

The man from the picture was smiling down at him.

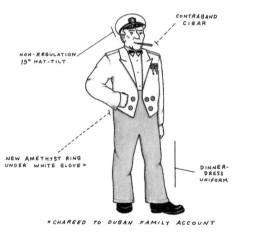

CONTRABAND CIGAR

NON-REGULATION 15° HAT-TILT

THE ADMIRAL

NORFOLK, VIRGINIA

SEMI-RETIRED

NEW AMETHYST RING UNDER WHITE GLOVE *

DINNER-DRESS UNIFORM

* CHARGED TO DUGAN FAMILY ACCOUNT

"Handsome pipe you got there," the Admiral said.

Nice going, Chuck thought, feeling a coldness settle in the pit of his stomach. You were pushing it. Sitting out in the open like this -- you were asking for it. Now, my friend, he sighed, you GOT it. Your luck's just run out ...

Chuck rose to his feet. He felt sick.

He was in disguise.

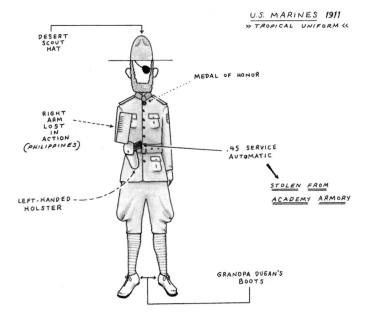

U.S. MARINES 1911
» TROPICAL UNIFORM «

DESERT
SCOUT
HAT

MEDAL OF HONOR

RIGHT
ARM
LOST
IN
ACTION
(PHILIPPINES)

.45 SERVICE
AUTOMATIC

STOLEN FROM
ACADEMY ARMORY

LEFT-HANDED
HOLSTER

GRANDPA DUGAN'S
BOOTS

Are you aware of your escape routes? he asked himself. Are you prepared to return fire? -- Or, if

necessary, initiate the action? With a sober sense of
his own rocky condition, he decided that the answers
to these questions were undoubtedly No, no, and no.
He gave a shaky left-handed salute.

What a way to go, he thought grimly. End of a
campaign.

"At ease, Sarge," the Admiral boomed good-
naturedly. "A pleasure to have the Corps at my home.
What's your poison?" He waved for Chuck to sit.

Chuck blinked. "My poison?" He coughed. In an
old man's quavering voice he said: "Panama Canal."

"Make it two there, Deckhand," the Admiral said
to Brace, who'd been watching this encounter with a
growing sense of alarm. He spun on the butler with
a snarl. "Step lively, dammit!"

"Oh!" Brace cried.

The Admiral caught Brace by the lapels and lifted
him onto his toes. "Use the proper form of address,"
he hissed.

"Sorry, sir!" Brace said. "I mean ... 'Aye-aye,
Admiral!'"

The Admiral released him. "Shove off."

Brace hurried up the path toward the house, leaving Chuck alone with the Admiral.

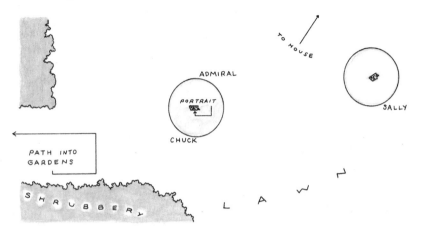

"May I join you? Sergeant ...?"

"<u>Bradshawe</u>," Chuck rasped. He gestured stiffly to the chair opposite his own.

"Panama Canal," the Admiral mused as he sat down. "That's a <u>sailor's</u> drink. How'd you come by the habit, old-timer?"

Chuck couldn't remember. He gave a shrug.

"Ah, well." The Admiral sighed contentedly. "It's a lovely night ... Pardon me, but your shirt is on fire. <u>This</u> <u>is</u> <u>not</u> <u>a</u> <u>drill</u>!"

Chuck glanced at his shirtfront. His lighter had set a small area smoking after being dropped, still lit, into an open pocket. He slapped the smoke out, grabbed his drink, and dumped it on himself. He froze. The fire had been put out, all right, but another one had started.

In responding to the crisis, he'd used his right arm.

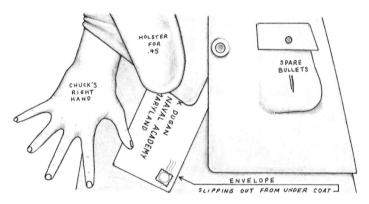

The Admiral was staring at Chuck through narrowed eyes. "I can't help noticing," he said quietly, "that you've grown a healthy right arm since we sat down."

Chuck sat perfectly still.

"Who are you?" the Admiral asked. "Her uncle? What have you heard about me?"

Chuck said nothing.

The Admiral sighed. "See here, old man. I have

a right to know what goes on under my own roof. Any subterfuge or hocus-pocus --"

"It _isn't_ your roof," Chuck said.

The Admiral smiled. "If you insist. As of tomorrow, however, it _will_ be mine. If you're here to protect your interests, I can understand that, old man. We should have a talk. However, if you'd come to me without the hidden agenda, I'd be more inclined to hear your list of grievances. As it is --"

A woman's raised voice interrupted the conversation:

"Did you assault my butler, you?!"

Chuck and the Admiral leaned away from the table to see Fraunces Dugan, Chuck's mother, standing in front of them, a furious expression on her face.

A portrait of Fraunces hung in the second-floor hall.

"Kindly wait until we're finished, dear," the Admiral said, an artificial smile pasted on his face.

"I will not have you terrorizing my help!" she continued. "Mr. Brace is like a member of the family!" Her English accent, though tempered by time, was still strong -- she'd grown up in Kent, by the sea. Brace and her father had fought side by side on the Western Front.

"And I," the Admiral said quietly, "will not be telling you again."

"You won't ... _what_?" She sounded horrified. "How dare you speak to me that way!"

The Admiral got to his feet. "Madam," he said coldly, "I have tolerated so much guff from you over the past two weeks, it would have busted the Captain of a Missile Destroyer down to Seaman First Class in Charge of Latrines."

Chuck was sweating. He shifted uneasily in his chair. Now, he told himself, would be a smart time to make a break for it.

Just then, Stretch Reilly and Harry Aloha came running down the hill from the house.

"Sorry, Dad!" Stretch gasped, pointing at

Fraunces. "Bloody woman gave us the slip!"

Fraunces scowled at the two boys. "May I ask why your sons see the need to follow me every place I go?"

"Have they bothered you?"

"Well, no," she said, her tone softening. "But that's not the point. It's almost as if -- well, as if you were having me watched!"

"I told you," the Admiral said, rubbing his eyes. "They're here for your own protection --"

"Because of your work for the government," she said. "Yes, you've explained all that. Not very convincingly, I might add." She glanced at Chuck. "Oh, pardon me, sir. I'm sorry to interrupt. Look, Admiral ..."

Shocked to hear his mother use the term "Admiral," Chuck turned in his seat and scrutinized the man. How, he wondered, had this crazy state of affairs come about? What strange power does the man possess? How can I bring Mom to her senses?

The table was suddenly quiet. Chuck looked up. His mother was staring into his face.

She had recognized him.

HOLY MACKEREL! Chuck jumped up and moved several paces to the left. Then several paces to the right. He stayed in motion -- back, left, right -- because his mother had an eye condition that had left her with very poor peripheral vision.

He knew this and tried to take advantage of it.

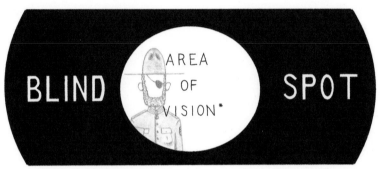

BLIND AREA OF VISION* SPOT

* FRAUNCES MAY NOT OPERATE MOTOR VEHICLES AFTER SUNSET

Meanwhile, he kept up a steady smokescreen of talk. "Not at all, dear girl ... pleasure to meet the lady of the house ... quite an island you have here ... perhaps you'd like to give an old Marine the nickel tour, hmm? ... how does that sound?"

She focused on Chuck's fingertips, sticking out from under the jacket ... the empty sleeve ... the Medal of Honor ... the false beard. She looked her son in the eye.

He winked at her.

"Chuck Dugan," she said, blowing his cover to smithereens, "go to your room this instant."

Chuck sighed heavily and drew the .45 automatic from its holster. "All right. Nobody move."

Brace arrived with the drinks.

"Panama Canals, gentlemen." He set them on the table, then noticed the gun in Chuck's left hand. His tray thudded to the ground. His expression darkened. "Well," the butler growled. "About time someone pulled a gun around here!" He picked up the Admiral's drink and raised it. "Confusion to our enemies," he declared, and drained the glass.

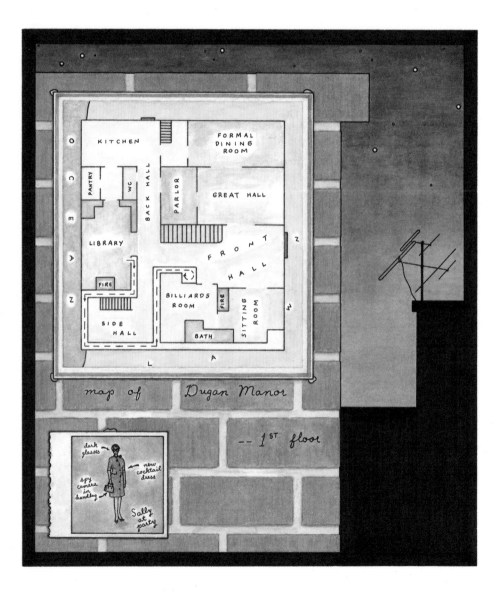

OCEAN

KITCHEN

FORMAL DINING ROOM

PANTRY

WC

BACK HALL

PARLOR

GREAT HALL

LIBRARY

FRONT HALL

FIRE

BILLIARDS ROOM

FIRE

SITTING ROOM

SIDE HALL

BATH

N

W

L

A

map of Dugan Manor

-- 1ST floor

dark glasses

new cocktail dress

spy camera in handbag

Sally at party

*** Chapter Six ***

ROOFTOP LAUNCH

At her nearby table, Sally strained to understand what was being said.

"Chuck!" Fraunces cried. "What in <u>Heaven's</u> name are you doing?"

"So," the Admiral said. "You're Chuck Dugan, are you?" He smiled. "We spoke on the telephone, if you recall."

Sally peered at the elderly Marine. Could it really be Chuck?

"Yessir," Chuck said. "You threatened to kill me if I showed up at my mother's wedding or in any way attempted to contact her. Thanks for the warning."

It _was_ Chuck.

"Not at all. You're an interesting boy." The Admiral chuckled good-naturedly. "What gives you the right to pull a gun on my lads?"

"I'm pulling the gun on _you_, Admiral. Brace --" Chuck turned to the trusted old butler standing beside him "-- will you please cover these men while I call the Shore Patrol?"

"With pleasure, Master Charles."

Chuck handed the pistol to the butler.

"Has everyone gone stark-raving mad?" Fraunces asked in a shrill tone.

"Mom, I'll explain later."

"Ah, well," the Admiral said pleasantly. "Maybe it's all for the best, Fraunces. Now you can see for yourself how badly the boy needs psychiatric help."

Chuck grunted, said, "I'll be right back" -- and stumbled.

Stretch reached out to grab Chuck's elbow.

"Get back!" Brace said, leveling the pistol at Stretch, who shrugged and moved away.

Sally saw the move -- _quick_ _as_ _lightning_.

SPY
CAMERA
VIEWFINDER

STRETCH'S
FINGERS

The envelope sticking out from under Chuck's coat vanished.

Moving briskly up the hill toward the house, past tables filled with elegant guests, Chuck sighed to himself. Home at last, he thought. Warm yellow light poured from the open windows. Music was in the air. Now where's the nearest telephone?

He passed through the open front door and down the hall to the library.

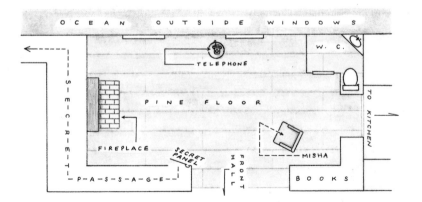

He moved past the figure seated in the armchair opposite the fireplace and went straight to the telephone. He picked it up and joggled the receiver.

"Operator? Get me Hammersmith 4-2-3. The U.S. Navy base at Topalian."

He heard nothing. The line was -- dead? Or had it been cut?

"Operator ...?"

Movement from the corner of his eye -- <u>Misha</u>! The Russian was crossing toward him, right hand glinting gold: <u>brass knuckles</u>. Chuck threw the phone at him. He dodged across the library and yanked Audubon's <u>Maritime Birds of New England</u> from the shelf, engaging the secret panel, swung it open, jumped inside, and slammed it shut behind him.

WHAM!

Misha hurled himself against the heavy iron latch, but the door to this secret passage was one of the strongest in the entire house.

Chuck hurried down the passage, as familiar to him as his own face, twisting and turning in the dark. He found a spiral staircase and hustled up as quick as he could. The one thought rushing through his

mind -- apart from the unforgivable stupidity
he'd shown in assuming his long ordeal had ended
-- was:

They can't have disconnected ALL the phones.
THEY need a phone. What's your best option?

He had it:

Second-Floor Staff Linen Closet. Move it!

The secret passage on the second floor emerged
from behind a deep-sea diver's suit at the end of
the hall.

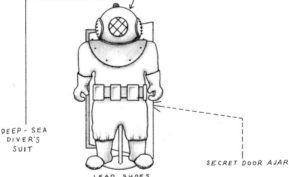

DEEP-SEA
DIVER'S
SUIT

SECRET DOOR AJAR

LEAD SHOES

Chuck jumped out the door and hurried down
the hallway. As he passed through the Staff Parlor,
he heard a distinct POP! outside.

The sound of a .45 automatic pistol firing.

He moved to the nearest window and looked down
at the lawn.

It could have been worse. Brace was lying on the ground, hand to head -- but alive. The Admiral's portrait that sat in the middle of the table had been shattered by the bullet. The Admiral himself, now holding Chuck's service automatic, passed the gun to Harry Aloha, who turned and sprinted up the hill to the house.

They really mean BUSINESS, Chuck thought.

He stepped away from the window, thinking, thinking ...

A shriek from the front door: now Harry, along with Misha, was inside the house.

And that, Chuck thought, is one too many for my taste. He sighed, took a deep breath, and plunged back into action. He dashed to the Staff Linen Closet, picked up the phone inside

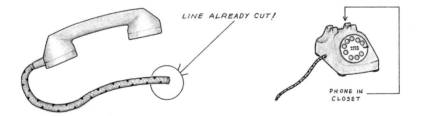

LINE ALREADY CUT!

PHONE IN CLOSET

and slammed it down. Ran up the hall to the deep-sea diver's suit, swung the door behind it open, dove back in while catching a glimpse of Harry Aloha coming up the main stairs. Harry -- seeing Chuck -- squeezed off a round from the .45.

CRUNCH!

Splinters rained across Chuck's back. He could have predicted what would come next.

SMAASH!

The Hawaiian burst through the door: the secret passage a secret no more.

You better come up with a fresh angle, Chuck told himself, running up the stairs. Or you're never gonna leave this party alive.

He arrived on the fourth floor, top floor of Dugan Manor. Here the staircase ended, and Chuck left the secret passage behind.

Sneezing as he hustled through Auntie Lorraine's room, he came upon a final set of steps that led to the roof. Chuck decided what he had to do, and it was simple: ESCAPE. Fight another day. He clambered up the steps, punched open the door, and stood on the roof in the cool night air.

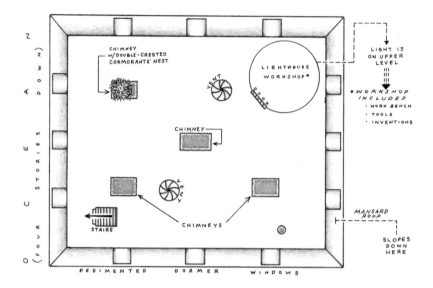

Inside the Lighthouse Workshop, Chuck found
a SCUBA tank. It held no air, but he wanted it for
ballast, so he shrugged into it. Then he lifted a
bicycle off its hooks. He threw a leg over the crossbar,
sat on the saddle -- and froze.

He was no longer alone on the roof.

Harry and Misha were near the opposite edge,
arguing about where Chuck had gone.

Time to do it, Chuck told himself, or retire
from the field.

This is what he was driving:

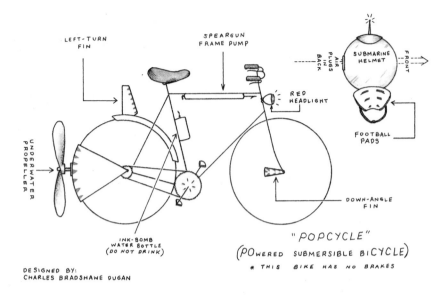

"POPCYCLE"
(POwered SUBMERSIBLE BiCYCLE)
* THIS BIKE HAS NO BRAKES

DESIGNED BY:
CHARLES BRADSHAWE DUGAN

Chuck licked a finger and held it out the door. Wind from the northeast. Good, he thought. The added lateral thrust will help me avoid hitting the side of the house on my way down.

Despite everything, he couldn't help feeling excited: it was the bike's maiden voyage. He wished he had a bottle of champagne.

Solemnly, he lifted the submarine helmet off the handlebars and put it on his head.

A deep breath: TEN ... NINE ...

"Check the lighthouse. There he is, Harry! Shoot him --!"

EIGHTSEVENSIXFIVEFOURTHREETWOONEGO!

Chuck pedaled like mad for the edge of the roof.

POP!

Dust flew off a chimney as he passed.

POP! ... POP! ...

Bullets whacked into the rooftop.

Down on the lawn, guests looked up at the roof
with cries of alarm. A figure appeared. Riding a
bicycle, pedaling furiously. Pedaling as he took the
down-sloping mansard roof's edge, pedaling for dear
life, hanging onto the handlebars, accelerating
through the air, down, down, in a frightening arc
to the inky water below -- where the bike literally
burst into a thousand pieces.

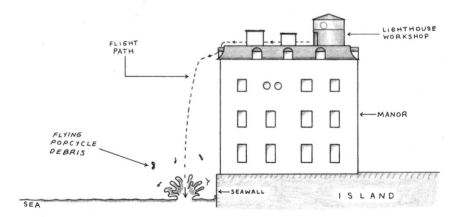

"That boy," the Admiral observed, "just broke his silly neck."

He was staring out at the water with a curious, bemused expression.

"You all right, sir?" Stretch asked. He and the Admiral were now alone at their table.

"Fine," the Admiral answered quietly, sipping the remains of Chuck's leftover drink, watching the party unravel.

"Dad."

The Admiral turned.

"What is it, son?"

"You'd better have a look at this, sir."

The two of them hunched over the table, where some documents were spread.

"Where'd you get these, son?"

"The boy had 'em. Hidden in an envelope under his coat."

The Admiral read the Letter grinning. He unfolded the Map and chuckled with delight, slapping his son on the shoulder. This was good. This was <u>better</u> than community property. He had what he wanted.

Or soon would.

*** Chapter Seven ***

OTHER BUSINESS

Early the following morning, Sally stood on the
front doorstep, waiting. She was in uniform again;
once more, she carried her Specimen Case.

Two minutes passed.

She rang the front doorbell. Nobody answered.
"Hello?" She knocked on the door.

A crab touched her foot. Moving across the grass.
Thinking food -- or the ocean -- lay this way. Though

fast in shallow waters, it was a slow creature on land: Callinectes sapidus -- the Blue Crab.

"You sick or something?" she asked. She picked it up.

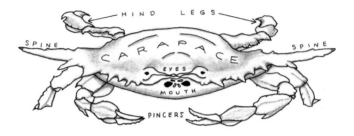

After carrying the crab by its shell down to the dock, Sally leaned over the water and returned it to its rightful habitat with a plunk!

Turning back to the house, she found Brace standing on the front doorstep.

"Good morning," she called and waved. She started back up the hill.

The tables from the night before all stood in the same place. Confetti, streamers, and cocktail glasses were being pecked by seagulls. What was to have been a celebration now felt gloomy and sad.

"How's the head?" she asked.

"Knitting admirably, miss," Brace replied.

It was an understatement, of course.

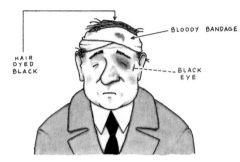

HAIR DYED BLACK

BLOODY BANDAGE

BLACK EYE

CLAUDE BRACE

BUTLER

72 YEARS OLD

"I'm here to see Chuck --"

He was blocking the door. "Midshipman Dugan is ... indisposed, miss."

"All right," she said. "I can wait."

He crossed his arms over his chest.

"Look, Mr. Brace," she said with a sigh. "I didn't come here to make trouble. I just want to see my friend. OK?"

He stared at her for a moment, weighing this remark, then opened the door wide.

The windows of the house had all been thrown open to allow in the fresh morning breeze. Curtains rustled. Timbers creaked and groaned. Sally looked around. It was very quiet.

"How is everything?" she asked.

"Calm, miss."

"Where's the Admiral?"

"Out of the picture, miss. He and his, ah -- family -- departed yesterday evening."

"Anything since?"

"Not a word." He stopped. For once, his courtesy seemed to fail him. "I'm ... rather busy, miss. Would you mind showing yourself the way?"

"Fine."

"Do you have any reservations against using the service stairs?"

"None whatsoever."

"Very good, miss."

He rapped his knuckles -- tocktock! -- on the wall beside them, and a spring-loaded panel popped free; a dim staircase was revealed inside.

"If you would be so good as to follow these to the third floor, miss, and exit where you see the portrait of Viscount Nelson ..."

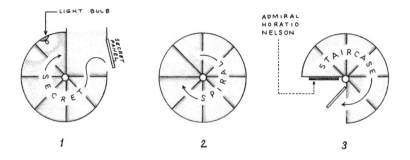

"Oh!" Fraunces said, seeing Sally appear. "It's you, Sally!" She cocked an eyebrow. "Doctor Adams," she said, "this is ... <u>Ensign</u> <u>Sally</u> <u>Wisebadger</u>." Her emphasis was odd.

Sally shook hands with the white-haired doctor. "Nice to meet you," she said.

"And you," he said softly, looking up at her. His grasp was very weak. He was about ninety.

Fraunces's voice was anxious. "Sally, I'm afraid Chuck is asleep."

"Why don't I wake him up?"

"Er -- no! That is ..."

"Out of the question," the doctor said, shaking his head. "The boy cannot be disturbed at present. He has a serious concussion. In fact, the boy ... is ... in a coma."

Sally nudged Chuck's door with her toe. It swung open. "Doctor Adams," she said. "Your patient has made a miraculous recovery."

"Oh dear," Fraunces said.

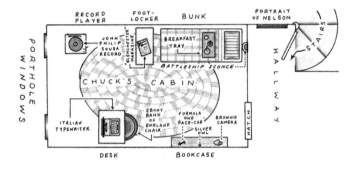

Chuck looked up. He was having breakfast in bed. He waved his spoon. "Hello all," he said.

Fraunces stepped into the room. "<u>Must</u> you take him to jail, Sally?"

"Mrs. Dugan --"

"Fraunces."

"I'm not here to arrest anybody." That is, she thought, not YET anyway. "It's true, I was sent up from Annapolis to try and get Chuck to come back to school with me. But it's his life."

"Hear-hear," Chuck said.

"Thank goodness!" Fraunces said.

Sally knelt by Chuck's bed, opened her case, and took out her stethoscope. Chuck winced as she pressed the cold metal to his bare chest. "So," she asked, "how do you feel?"

"Good," he answered.

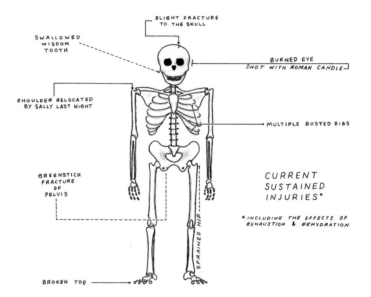

SLIGHT FRACTURE
TO THE SKULL

SWALLOWED
WISDOM
TOOTH

BURNED EYE
SHOT WITH ROMAN CANDLE

SHOULDER RELOCATED
BY SALLY LAST NIGHT

MULTIPLE BUSTED RIBS

GREENSTICK
FRACTURE
OF
PELVIS

CURRENT
SUSTAINED
INJURIES*

*INCLUDING THE EFFECTS OF
EXHAUSTION & DEHYDRATION

SPRAINED HIP

BROKEN TOE

Sally shook her head. "Chuck, you belong in the hospital."

He laughed. "They were afraid I'd get arrested."

"Ahem." A voice at the door. They looked up.

"Telephone call," Brace said. He held a phone on his tray, connected by a long cord that trailed out the door and down the hall.

"For whom?"

"Master Charles, ma'am. The Admiral calling."

Stunned silence.

"The <u>Admiral</u>!" Fraunces cried.

"For Chuck?" Sally asked.

"Yes, miss."

Chuck raised his hand. "I'll take it."

"Very good, sir."

He carried the phone over. Chuck picked up the receiver.

"This is Chuck."

A pause.

"Yeah, I'm still alive, Admiral. Bad luck. Maybe next time you'll --" The blood drained from Chuck's face.

He cupped his hand over the receiver. "<u>Brace</u>!" he hissed. "<u>My</u> <u>uniform</u> <u>from</u> <u>last</u> <u>night</u> -- <u>where</u> <u>is</u> <u>it</u>?"

"Being laundered, sir."

"An envelope was inside the jacket -- you didn't wash it, did you?"

"No, sir."

Chuck heaved a sigh of relief. "Thank --"

"I didn't find any envelope, sir."

Chuck, horrified, stared at the butler.

The line went dead.

Sally sighed heavily. And now, she thought, for the other business. She reached inside her case and brought out a short stack of photographs, which she set in a neat pile on Chuck's breakfast tray.

"What on earth is going on?" Fraunces asked.

Chuck's eyes swam down to the photographs. "What're these?"

"You tell me, Chuck."

He lifted the first photo -- and laughed triumphantly.

"You've got it, Sally!"

"Read it out to everyone, Chuck," Sally said.

He had to squint to make out the words.

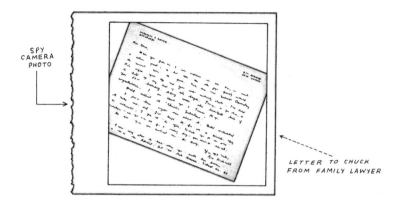

SPY CAMERA PHOTO

LETTER TO CHUCK FROM FAMILY LAWYER

"Have you seen the Map that goes with it?"
Chuck asked.

"Next picture down," Sally said.

Chuck examined the photograph of the Treasure
Map.

"Why was the Admiral calling?" Fraunces asked.
"What did he want? What did he say?"

"He said he stole my Map," Chuck said. "But it
was just a bluff. Sally has it."

"Chuck, I have <u>photos</u>."

"You ..." He stared at Sally. "Wait a second.
You <u>gotta</u> have it. How else could you --"

"Turn to the last picture."

Wincing in pain, Chuck slid out of his bunk and limped to his desk, one hand pressed to his aching back. Everyone watched as he began putting his shoes back on. He strapped his buck-knife to his belt, put the eye patch in its place over his injured left eye.

"Mom," he said. "Where's the boat?"

Fraunces blinked. "The boat? Why ... it's ... at the boatwright's, dear. Blown crankshaft."

"I need it."

"Today is Sunday. They're closed."

He nodded to himself. "They're about to open up."

Sally said: "What boat?"

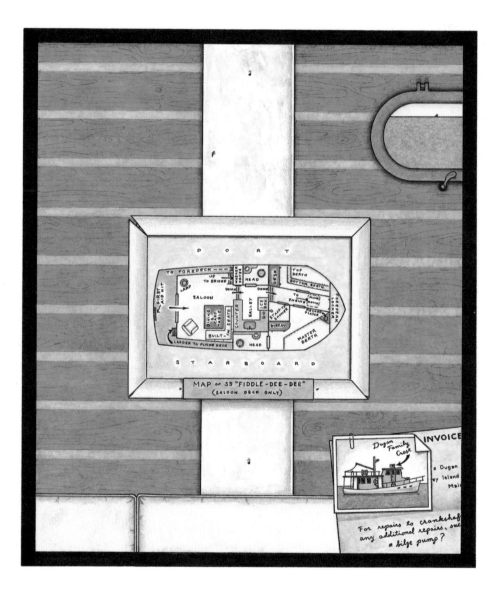

✳✳✳ Chapter Eight ✳✳✳
THE FIDDLE-DEE-DEE

Chuck dropped from the chain-link fence onto the wooden dock. Slowly he rose to his full height.

"Roscoe," he called softly. He was tense, listening. The place was quiet. He whistled. "Here, boy."

Shifting his gaze, he took in the long dock of the boatwright's yard, the water beyond the fence, and the boats anchored in the pond.

Nobody home.

Brace was standing on the other side of the fence, next to a pair of bicycles. He held a dogcatcher's net in his hands. "Sir, perhaps there has been some personnel shift, resulting in --"

A dog trotted around the corner of the boathouse. Chuck held his breath.

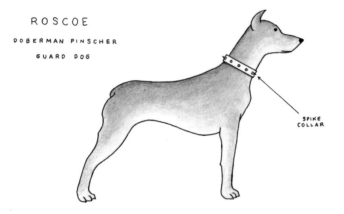

ROSCOE
DOBERMAN PINSCHER
GUARD DOG

SPIKE
COLLAR

That animal, he thought, has grown since the last time I saw him.

"The net, sir!" Brace whispered. "Before it's too late!"

The dog, seeing them, burst into a gallop, barking viciously, racing straight up the dock.

Hold still, Chuck told himself.

Stand your ground.

Hear its breathing ... NOW!

Chuck took a leather sap

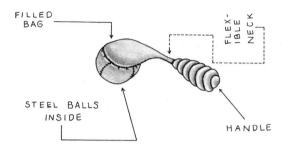

FILLED BAG

FLEXIBLE NECK

STEEL BALLS INSIDE

HANDLE

from behind his back and hit the dog as hard as he could on the nose with it.

The dog bashed into the fence, howling in pain, then picked itself up and stood shivering on the dock, looking dazed.

"Sorry, Roscoe," Chuck said. "I had to do it." He unlocked the gate.

"A pity, sir." Brace stepped inside and examined the dog. It whined and licked his face. He fed it some licorice. In addition to his usual black suit, the butler now wore a fisherman's hat and yellow boaters on his feet.

"Where to, sir?" he asked, straightening.

Chuck pointed his chin at the end of the dock. "The boathouse." They began walking.

"Nice morning for a treasure hunt, sir."

Chuck grunted. He didn't like the look of that sky.

A moment later, the dog followed, gnawing on its piece of licorice.

"What about petrol, sir?"

"We'll gas her up at Ferrygate."

They reached the boathouse and kicked the door in.

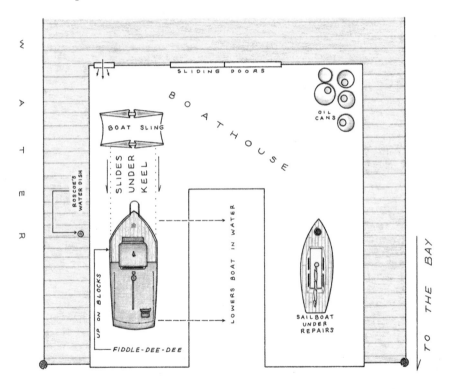

Half an hour later, they had the boat in the water, engine puttering.

"I believe the animal wishes to accompany us, sir."

Chuck looked back to see Roscoe standing on the fantail. He shook his head. "No dogs allowed."

From the safety of the dock, Roscoe watched as the <u>Fiddle</u>-<u>Dee</u>-<u>Dee</u> motored out of the boatwright's yard and headed into Technical Bay. A few minutes after that, they came to Ferrygate Wharf.

"Let's make this quick," Chuck said, eyeing the Harbor Master's office uneasily. "I had some trouble here yesterday."

"Hi," Sally said. "You made good time." She and Fraunces were unloading Chuck's station wagon, stacking equipment on the dock.

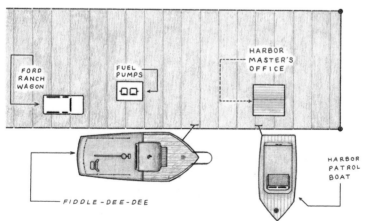

An officer of the Sheriff's Department stood nearby, smoking a cigarette. Chuck waved. The officer waved back. Then frowned to himself. He stubbed out his cigarette, turned, and stepped aboard the Harbor Patrol vessel that was tied up to the dock.

Not good, Chuck thought. "Brace," he said, "we need to leave here in less than three minutes, if possible."

"I'm coming too," his mother said, carrying equipment onto the boat.

"What?" Chuck was caught off-guard. "No, you're not."

"Try and stop me." She stepped past him.

Chuck shook his head. Too slow, he told himself, watching her go below. Well, at least she's an above-average sailor.

He began lifting and carrying gear onboard. SCUBA tank ... another SCUBA tank ... a box of flares ... two pairs of fins. One case slipped from his arms and banged onto the deck. Its contents scattered. He stooped to collect them, then paused.

Spy camera ... fingerprint powder ... mini-tape recorder ...

It was Sally's Specimen Case. He hurriedly raked all the loose objects together and made a pile.

One item stood out.

Knuckles turning white, Chuck gripped the packet in his hands, staring fiercely at its bright red exterior. He was hypnotized. With slow, precise movements, he reached for the emergency kit that was attached to a nearby bulkhead. Slowly he opened it. Slowly he shoved the packet inside, next to the flare gun and the waterproof matches. Slowly he closed it shut again.

He stared numbly at the deck. My friend, he told himself, you have just committed a federal crime. His face tingled. He felt nauseous. You are now a SPY.

He gathered the things up and returned them to Sally's case. Then he shut, locked, and carried the case below with the rest of the gear.

His mother, seeing the expression on Chuck's face, stopped what she was doing. "How are you feeling?" She sounded worried. She put a hand to his head. "You're not feverish?"

"No ... fine." He stared into space. "Please man the helm."

Chuck wandered back on deck. He took in the view of the wharf as if for the first time that day. Everything seemed silent and watchful. It gave him an uneasy feeling. He tilted his head, observing the clear, sharp quality of the light. Storm weather? he wondered. Or is it just me? A bird, passing overhead, gave a squawk! Chuck jumped.

What the hell is going on here? he asked himself, rubbing his chin absently. His thoughts were a muddle. I need a shave ...

CLUNK!

The pump shut off. Sally, finished refueling the boat, returned the nozzle to the pump stand and went inside the Harbor Master's office to pay for it.

"Start the engines," Chuck said to his mother. Then he shouted: "Mr. Brace!"

Brace appeared on deck. "Sir?"

"Prepare to repel boarders."

Brace blinked at him. "How?"

Chuck realized full well he was wanted for questioning about the incident on the ferry yesterday. Not to mention assaulting the Harbor Master. Not to mention being AWOL.

"You got anything on hand we can throw?"

"Throw, sir?"

He spotted Sally backing her way out of the Harbor Master's office, talking steadily, her hands raised, placating.

He caught her attention and mouthed:

L - E - T - S ... G - O ...

She nodded:

A-F-F-I-R-M-A-T-I-V-E.

"Yeah, <u>throw</u>," Chuck repeated. "My gun was stolen. What's in the basket?"

Brace had packed a picnic lunch for the expedition.

"Sandwiches, sir. A thermos. Cake."

"Well get me <u>something</u>, man."

Brace disappeared below.

Sally ran for the boat and leapt aboard. At that moment, the police officer emerged from the Harbor Patrol boat and began walking down the dock toward them.

"Cast all lines free!" Chuck shouted.

"Wait a minute," the policeman said. "I need to talk to you folks."

"Full speed ahead! Repel boarders!"

The officer took a dozen quick steps in their direction. Brace appeared with an armload of apples.

THE <u>EARLY JOE</u> HAS
A THIN SKIN BUT A
FINE, ROBUST FLAVOR

He and Chuck began pitching fastballs. The
policeman ducked. The engines roared.

They were clear.

*** Chapter Nine ***

EMERGENCY RESCUE BUOY NO. 49

Chuck was thinking about ten things at once.
Foremost: a plan was needed. They were about to be
chased.

He was -- automatically -- the Captain.

"Nice work, everybody."

They were whipping across the Bay, plowing and
leaping the waves.

Fraunces was at the helm, steering the boat, a
determined expression on her face.

"Are we being pursued, dear?" she asked.

He didn't need to glance at the radar. He
squinted aft. "Yep."

He leaned over a precise chart of the Bay. Poring over its details, searching for something special, something out of the way.

"OK," he said, straightening. He knew what to do. He slipped a pair of swimming goggles around his neck. "Here's the idea ..."

Moments later, the Fiddle-Dee-Dee drifted to a standstill, her engines quiet. They were dead in the water.

A siren split the air.

"Fiddle-Dee-Dee!" The Harbor Patrol boat had caught up with them and now lay idling off their stern. An officer spoke over a megaphone. "Heave-to and drop anchor. Everyone onboard come out with their hands up."

They complied, emerging on deck with arms raised high: Fraunces, Brace, and Sally.

"Where's the boy?" the officer asked.

Fraunces looked stunned, her face deathly pale. With a trembling hand, she pointed to the side of the boat.

"He --!" she choked. "He jumped overboard!"

"Again?" the officer asked.

FIDDLE-DEE-DEE

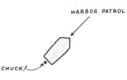

HARBOR PATROL

CHUCK!

Chuck hugged onto the tail of the police
boat, listening. His mother was giving a convincing
performance.

Dripping water, he climbed aboard and snuck
across the deck to the main, low-ceilinged cabin.
He stood at the doorway. A radio operator, wearing
headphones, was sitting with his back to him. Chuck
tip-toed to the forward hatch, carefully opened it
wide enough to enter, then closed it softly behind
him again.

He was in the engine space.

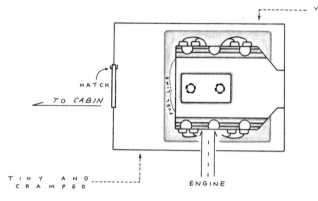

Chuck took out his buck-knife, unfolded the blade, and sliced the rubber fuel line in half. Immediately, a surge of fuel spilled across the floor, splattering his shoes. He turned to exit the way he'd come. But as he put his hand to the door, he heard voices on the other side.

Men were in the cabin.

Chuck groaned. This was a lousy place to be trapped. An overwhelming stench of gas fumes rose up, filling the tiny chamber. He clamped his arm over his mouth and pinched his nostrils shut, trying not to smell it, trying not to <u>breathe</u>, even though it would mean suffocation.

He felt disgusted with himself. The clock was ticking -- and here he was. "The Captain." Trapped.

Captain? He sneered. What kind of a Captain brings his <u>butler</u> on a mission? Or, for that matter, his <u>mom</u>?

He shook his head, as much to drive away the negative train of thought as to keep himself from losing consciousness. He was not a defeatist. But the air was poison.

Gasoline was bubbling thick across the deck when -- with a clap of thunder! -- the engines coughed to life and immediately went to FULL, chugging away, rattling the decks, making Chuck spin around and grip the bulkhead with both hands, expecting disaster at any moment.

His mother, he knew, had just made a dash for it. The Sheriff's boat, caught off-guard, was now chasing the <u>Fiddle</u>-<u>Dee</u>-<u>Dee</u>, racing across the sea.

Slowly, Chuck took a step forward and stared at the engine, pumping away like mad. It had turned into a potential bomb. If you see a spark, he warned himself, slap it out quick!

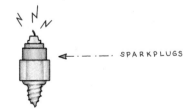

SPARKPLUGS

He didn't breathe. His eyes were everywhere at once. The air itself was flammable. If a spark came off the engine, the boat would explode -- with all these men onboard. He'd put their lives at risk. Men with families.

Thirty long seconds passed. No sparks -- yet.

The motor sputtered.

And now, Chuck told himself, you need to get OUT OF HERE.

The engine died. Out of fuel. He heard pounding feet from the flying bridge above.

He turned and opened the hatch a crack. The cabin was empty. The vessel was slowing.

Now's your chance. He flung the hatch open.

A policeman, sitting in a chair, was loading his revolver. He looked up in surprise. "Hey --"

Chuck ran past him, out the door. The fresh air tasted sweet; he inhaled it greedily.

"Heyyouguysthatkidjust --!"

Chuck dove headlong into the boat's wake.

Cool water surrounded him instantly ... flowed over him, numbing weary muscles, washing away the stink of gasoline, blotting out the troubles of the

surface world. Chuck jack-knifed to <u>port</u> -- that
was due east -- and continued his dive, going deeper
and deeper.

His arms and legs were working steadily. His mind
was clear. He was back in his element. He continued
to descend.

This trip, he estimated, should take me thirty
minutes. He began rising. With any luck, they'll be
there waiting for me.

He reached the surface and swam on.

Emergency Rescue Buoy No. 49 was located a
mile offshore. It had an inner chamber where a small
group of people could weather a bad storm or escape
a sinking ferry. At the very least, it was dry and
outfitted with a meager store of supplies.

Chuck had been to No. 49 on a number of
occasions. Never in an emergency, just as a place to
swim to, a novel destination. He'd chosen it now for
its unexpectedness as a rendezvous.

A dull-sounding CLANK! told him he was getting
close.

It would make a good hide-out, No. 49. He could
lie up there for a while or even wait until dark. But

that, he had told the others, would be nothing short of disastrous. He'd insisted upon the need for quick action.

Now he spotted the friendly orange buoy, bobbing on the waves.

He grabbed ahold of the ladder rungs bolted to the side -- CLANK! went the rusty bell -- then climbed onto the buoy's thin metal lip, slapping his body dry. Turning, shoes full of water, he looked back at the faint green haze that was the coast of Maine. He gave a sigh. No-one in sight.

Not good news. Not bad news.

The sudden breeze made him shiver. A voice in his mind asked: Why?

He frowned, remembering the red packet. The one marked TOP SECRET.

Why Budd? Why Assassination? WHY?

Chuck felt scared. None of my business. It was a mistake to take it -- a security breach. I'll return it as soon as I get back.

He cranked open the scarred hatch and descended the ladder into the buoy's iron stomach.

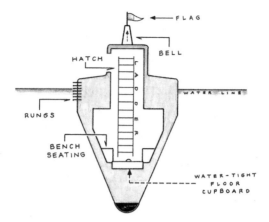

Dark and cold, but reasonably dry, he was surprised to find a towel. By the faint glimmer of reflected sunlight, Chuck opened the water-tight cupboard and made an inventory.

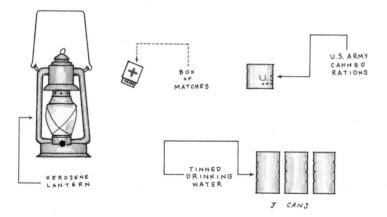

There wasn't a can opener anywhere.

With his knife, Chuck hacked two holes in one of the cans of water, then opened some franks-and-beans. The water tasted like rust. He lit the lantern, draped himself in the towel, and sat down to eat.

The franks-and-beans were unexpectedly good. He ate with his fingers. He decided he could have been in the Army. He leaned back, to stretch his sore neck, and was instantly asleep.

A faint grumble woke him. He hoped it wasn't thunder. He climbed the ladder to the surface.

The day had turned sunny and hot. There wasn't a cloud in the sky, just a strong northerly breeze.

The buoy sloshed from side to side. Chuck clenched the ladder. Incoming traffic. He stepped out the rest of the way to see.

The others gave a cheer when they saw Chuck emerge, blinking, into the sunlight. It was the Fiddle-Dee-Dee.

"Good morning, dear!" Fraunces called.

"What time is it?" Chuck asked.

"Ten-thirty!"

They were doing well.

Chuck went below, dowsed the lantern, tidied the place up, and quickly returned to the surface.

The boat steered close and nudged the buoy. Chuck hopped aboard.

"Helmsman, make your direction oh-four-five degrees," he yelled. "All ahead full."

"Nice job!" Sally said. She grinned and patted him on the back.

Chuck, about to speak, remembered what he had hidden in the emergency kit. Frowning, he turned away.

"Thanks," he mumbled.

They headed northeast.

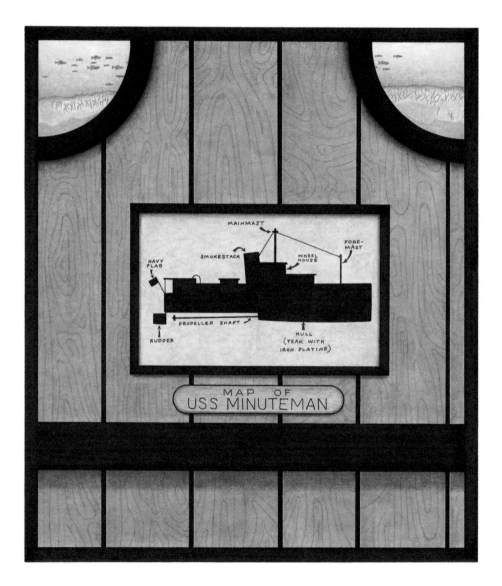

MAINMAST

SMOKESTACK

FORE-
MAST

NAVY
FLAG

WHEEL
HOUSE

PROPELLER SHAFT

RUDDER

HULL
(TEAK WITH
IRON PLATING)

MAP OF
USS MINUTEMAN

*** Chapter Ten ***
TOO LATE

With a heavy splash, Chuck fell backward off the
boat, holding his mask to his face.

The water was placid and amazingly clear: crisp
indigo in every direction. The mid-day sun was shining
directly overhead, and shafts of light rippled in the
gentle current.

He drifted downward.

A second, muffled splash -- and Sally floated
into position beside him. They turned to look at each
other and exchanged the standard greeting: O.K.

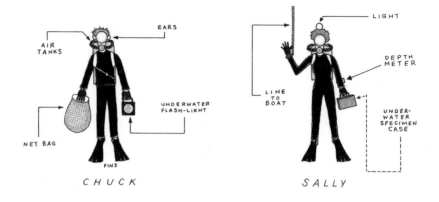

CHUCK

SALLY

They began their dive, confident that they had anchored in the right spot.

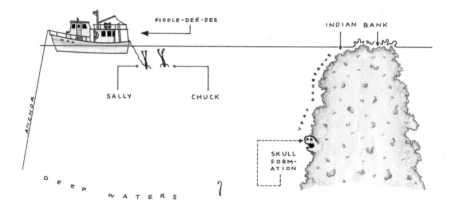

Indian Bank was not visible above the water, but it was massive underneath, like a decapitated iceberg of treacherous coral. Finding it had not been easy; hitting it would have ripped their boat apart. If they had reached the proper co-ordinates -- and found the final resting place of the <u>Minuteman</u> -- it was through careful navigating.

TWENTY FEET, Sally signaled. She was watching the depth meter attached to her arm.

Chuck stared hard into the soup between his outstretched fingers and saw -- shadows. Tricks of the light. Possibly a school of tuna.

Although they'd made good time getting here and had met no troubles, they still remained cautious: a thin nylon twine ran down from the <u>Fiddle</u>-<u>Dee</u>-<u>Dee</u> and connected with Sally's right wrist. She'd invented a simple code for everyone to follow.

TUGS FROM THE BOAT:

<u>ONE</u>	<u>TWO</u>	<u>THREE</u>
IS ALL WELL?	MESSAGE. ONE DIVER SURFACE.	EMERGENCY! ALL DIVERS OUT!

TUGS FROM THE WATER:

<u>ONE</u>	<u>TWO</u>	<u>THREE</u>
ALL IS WELL.	STAND BY. OR REPEAT.	PULL US OUT!

Sally signaled: THIRTY FEET. HOW DO YOU FEEL?
Chuck gave her the O-K. It was not the truth. He

felt steady in the hands but not in the mind. That damn red packet, he thought uneasily. It continued to trouble him; he had never returned it.

Among the purple contours of Indian Bank to his left, something caught Chuck's eye. A naturally occurring formation. He'd seen it before.

On the Map:

SHAPE
OF
A
SKULL

CLIFF FACE

They were in the right place. <u>Had</u> to be. He gave Sally a wave. They halted, nodding at their good fortune. It was a smart idea to pause for a moment. In any dive, but particularly one to a depth of ...

Well, they didn't <u>know</u> how deep exactly. A chart of the area said it could be two hundred feet. Under those conditions, they'd be no better than fumbling in the dark. The ocean floor dropped off somewhere nearby. There was an underwater ravine. If they were lucky, the subchaser had settled on the cliff above the gully, in shallow waters -- and in one piece.

FORTY FEET.

Suddenly, Sally's arm was pointing straight down. Her eyes were opened wide, staring into the murky space below. Chuck gave the signal.

OK. LET'S HOLD STEADY.

He peered down. There was <u>something</u> down there ... a dark form ... difficult to make out. YES, I THINK THAT'S IT. LET'S GO.

NO, WAIT! The water around them shifted, and a long red tentacle reached up out of the gloom.

Before they could react, it attached itself to Chuck's oxygen tank. He stiffened, expecting to be dragged, but the arm, just as quickly as it had appeared, released the tank, rolled in on itself again, and vanished below.

Chuck and Sally exchanged a horrified look.

And now the massive thing from the deep rose into view, confronting them directly. All Chuck could remember afterward was seeing <u>himself</u>: suspended, trapped within the shiny sphere of its right eye.

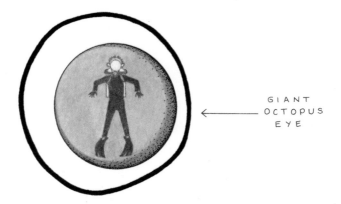

GIANT
OCTOPUS
EYE

The sea monster slithered close, taking them in with its enormous solemn gaze. It seemed bashful and inquisitive, its only hostility in its overwhelming bulk. Many tentacles reached out at once, their touch

light, probing -- puzzled by these two strange
creatures of metal and rubber.

But Chuck was alarmed. Behind all this soft,
curious contact, he knew there existed great danger
for them: the <u>snapping</u> <u>carnivorous</u> <u>beak</u>, hard as
iron, beneath the oblong head that led into its mouth.
This was no dolphin or sea lion they were playing
with. This was a hunter.

He flipped the switch on his flashlight and
aimed the beam into the eye.

The octopus reared up and shot away, leaving
them twirling in a cloud of jet-black ink.

The encounter was over.

Chuck's and Sally's hands were locked together
-- The Buddy System -- something their training made
them do instinctively. If the octopus had <u>attacked</u>,
the reasoning went, they would have to stick together.

The twine on her opposite wrist gave a twitch.

IS ALL WELL?

She replied with a single answering tug, telling
the boat:

EVERYTHING WELL.

Chuck and Sally looked into each other's face.

YOU ALL RIGHT?

O-K. HOW ARE YOU?

NEVER BETTER. THAT WAS SOMETHING.

INCREDIBLE.

LET'S KEEP GOING.

Sally nodded, and they floated downward, almost impaling themselves on the narrow wooden mainmast of the USS <u>Minuteman</u>.

Despite the number of things they could have been looking at, their attention focused on one detail only.

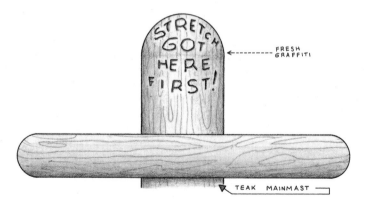

Disaster. They were too late.

WHAT DO WE DO?

GO IN ANYWAY. YOU TAKE FORWARD. I'LL TAKE AFT.

Chuck kicked hard, swimming down, trying to keep his disappointment in check. As he moved, he took in the full scope and size of the wreck, now visible beneath him.

Well, she'd sunk, the Minuteman had, but she hadn't blown up. Her timbers appeared to be in clean shape. Her smokestack was intact, the super-structure looked as good as new -- apart from all the barnacles, of course.

A notion occurred to Chuck. Maybe this alleged torpedoing never took place.

He brushed the sandy floor with his fins. He was now seventy feet below sea level. Before him, the ship lay stretched out, clean and untouched, like a model on someone's desk. A virtual museum piece.

Maybe, Chuck pondered, she foundered on Indian Bank. Why not? It sank plenty of good ships in its day.

But then he saw the hole: smack in her side. It was a torpedo, all right.

Punched through clean as a knife, he marveled, examining the breach in the thick wood and the outer shell of iron that coated the hull like a second skin. But it didn't detonate, he observed. If it had, that hole would have been the size of a tank. Well, this is as good a place as any ...

He swam in through the torpedo hole.

Now the dim available light left him entirely, and he was surrounded by cold black water.

The Map didn't say where the treasure was exactly: inside the wreck of the <u>Minuteman</u> -- that was all. A faint hope, in the back of Chuck's mind, was that the Admiral hadn't been able to find it. And had given up.

Or got devoured by the octopus.

The yellow circle from his flashlight was his

only illumination as he traveled forward. He did not lay his hand down unless he had to and was aware of what he was touching. From experience, he knew that many kinds of ordnance -- especially torpedoes, of which the <u>Minuteman</u> had been carrying at least a dozen -- could remain volatile for decades so long as the water didn't seep into the detonator housings. The last thing they needed was an accident.

He was also afraid of a boobytrap.

The warning never left his mind: The Admiral and his boys were down here.

In a typical dive, he and Sally would have remained together. But they'd planned in advance to split up once they reached the wreck. Not that it mattered now. They were too late. There was no --

Chuck saw his first dead sailor.

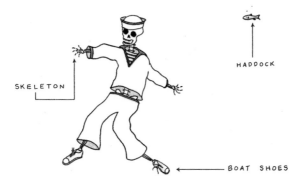

SKELETON

HADDOCK

BOAT SHOES

After staring at it for a moment, Chuck blinked in surprise. He was not seeing a dead American sailor -- which he'd naturally been expecting -- but a dead <u>German</u>. At least, the uniform was that of the German Navy. How was that possible? He drifted closer and confirmed it by the writing along the brim of the sailor's cloth hat.

What the hell was a dead German U-boat sailor doing onboard a sunk United States vessel? It was a mystery.

Chuck drifted forward, passing through various shorn bulkheads, catching glimpses of small chambers. The torpedo had wreaked havoc, causing tremendous damage. But not, he reminded himself, as much as if it had exploded. It had entered at an unlucky up-sloping angle, piercing walls and decks.

All the fail-safe measures had failed to cope with the torrent of incoming seawater -- and the boat just _sunk_. Probably within seconds.

Then he saw it.

The torpedo -- the killer of the _Minuteman_ and however many men she'd carried -- lay wedged inside a water purification tank. For all its force, a dud.

It made no difference, Chuck thought, staring at the menacing black cylinder. You got 'em anyway.

He shined his light back down the torpedo's destructive path.

What conclusions, he asked himself, would you draw if you were the one writing up the report on this disaster?

He answered the question without having to think.

Well, first of all, I'd take a look at that torpedo and figure out why in blazes it didn't blow up like it was supposed to.

He swam closer to it, and his blood ran cold.

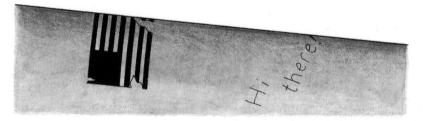

The torpedo was American.

Technical Islander December 14, 1941

REGATTA CHAMP GIVES YACHT TO NAVY
PRIVATE SHIP WILL BECOME SUBCHASER FOR DURATION

MAP OF MAINDECK

B. DUGAN, CHIEF DESIGNER   192

Technical Islander April 15, 1953

YACHTSMAN DIES IN MYSTERIOUS FIRE
OBSERVATORY DESTROYED
Fire Marshal: 'No Evidence of Arson'

TECHNICAL ISLAND
Mr. Budd Dugan,
49, of Chertsey, Maine,
died late yesterday in an

Apart from a sing
digit from the victim'
right hand, no remai
have yet been recove
Mr. Dugan has been li
as missing, presume

*** Chapter Eleven ***

IN THE DARK

Here, Chuck thought, is a clear sign of TREASON.

The wreck seemed to close in around him as he imagined the traitor ... going about his dark task, silently arranging the murder of his comrades.

Treason: the blackest crime at sea.

Chuck made a mental note to himself: Inform the Secretary of the Navy about this when it's all over.

He pulled a clear acetate sleeve out of his net bag. Inside was a plan of the ship. A blueprint of the <u>Autumn Harvest</u>, the name the ship bore when she was the Dugan family yacht. Before the War. Before his father had given it to the Navy to be refitted as a subchaser. He'd grown up with the blueprint hanging on his bedroom wall.

Now he had it sheathed in plastic.

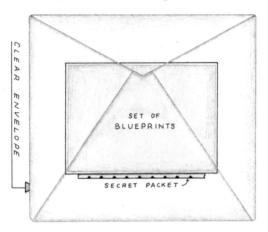

He couldn't help marveling at the situation he was in. Here he was, Chuck Dugan, exploring the <u>Autumn Harvest</u>, his dad's ship, which became the <u>Minuteman</u>, the Navy's ship, which was lost at sea nineteen years ago and never heard from since.

This, he told himself, is the week of ancient history coming back to life.

Now for the business at hand. The Treasure.

What would've been the likeliest place for Dad to hide it?

Chuck felt an idea tugging at him.

He traced his finger along the blueprint to the
maindeck level ... up the passage ... to the Stateroom.
He tapped a small area inside marked by the acronym
"SC." Chuck knew what that would stand for. Ever since
he was a little kid, he'd known of his father's
fondness for hidden doors and secret passages.

It must be there. SC. Secret Compartment.

He swam toward the ladder, floated to the top,
turned, and headed up the maindeck passageway.

He stopped where the Stateroom would be. The
plaque read: "Officers Mess." But Chuck was staring
at the condition of the door itself.

RECENTLY KICKED-IN
STATEROOM DOOR

Shaking his head regretfully, he swam inside,
noticing that, with the general list of the ship as it had
settled on the bottom, to go <u>in</u> he was actually going <u>up</u>.

Therefore, he was not surprised when he saw the water taper off into the opposite corner. It shimmered in the glow of his flashlight. An air pocket.

The ship had held together well enough that the air in this room -- or at least some of it -- had not been pushed out by the incoming water. There was a tight seal up there. And a small supply of oxygen.

THONK.

He looked back to see Sally emerge from the maindeck hall. She'd knocked to get his attention. She made a gesture with her arms that meant: EMPTY-HANDED -- she hadn't found anything. She pointed at the smashed-open door. Chuck nodded.

He moved to where the blueprint said the Secret Compartment should be. The basic layout of the ship was the same on his map as it was when it was converted into a subchaser; so when he saw the fresh marks of violence around the hidden panel -- splintered wood and torn-out hinges -- he knew that the Admiral had beaten them to it.

Sally joined him. They stared at the empty space wondering, with a mix of emotions, what might have been there. What marvels, what jewels ... For ten years -- until today.

Sally pointed to the air pocket above them. Chuck gave the O-K. They floated up and over, and their heads broke the surface at the same time.

Chuck removed his mouthpiece and shoved his mask to the top of his head.

He was bitterly disappointed. "They knew <u>exactly</u> where to look!"

"So it would seem," Sally answered. "The wreck is amazingly well preserved otherwise."

"Yeah, that's what I was thinking."

She nodded at the Secret Compartment.

"Obviously, from his firsthand knowledge of the ship, the Admiral guessed your father would hide the Treasure in there."

"What do you mean 'firsthand knowledge'?"

Sally frowned. "I thought you knew. The Admiral was in command of this subchaser."

"He ... was ... <u>what</u>?" Chuck turned away from her.

"Hey ..." she said after a moment. "You all right, Chuck?"

Chuck reached into his net bag for the acetate sleeve and removed the secret red packet he'd stolen from her that morning.

Sally's voice was cold. "<u>Where</u> <u>did</u> <u>you</u> <u>get</u> <u>that</u>?"

"It fell out of your case. I want you to explain something to me." From inside the red packet, he removed the following document and handed it to Sally:

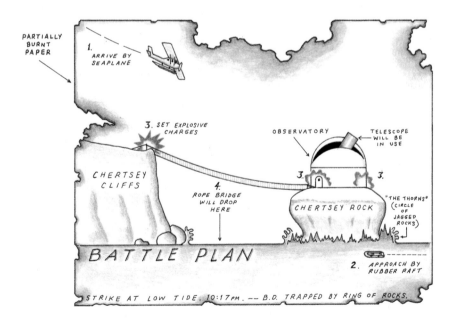

"You've been hiding things from me, Sally. Keeping me in the dark. That's no way to run a mission."

Sally's tone was adamant. "I cannot discuss classified --"

Chuck laid a hand on her arm. "Sally," he urged. "This document, whatever it means, is about my family."

She looked down at the worn, yellowed Battle Plan in her hands. It made her tired. The whole thing did. Sick and tired. She sighed. "Chuck, raise your right hand and repeat after me."

"What?"

"You're about to take an oath."

Chuck lifted his black-gloved hand into the stale, 1942 air and repeated the oath Sally invented on the spot:

"On my honor as a Naval Academy Midshipman, AWOL or otherwise, I swear I will not reveal classified information to anyone. Period."

Satisfied, Sally nodded. "Before graduation, I was recruited into Naval Intelligence."

Chuck rolled his eyes. "No kidding, Sally.

Everybody knew that."

"Well, what do you know," Sally continued, "about your father's work during the War?"

Chuck frowned. The question puzzled him. He knew what he knew. "Dad and Uncle Gus were POWs in Burma."

"Anything else?"

"President Eisenhower sent me a telegram on my tenth birthday."

"Mm-hmm. Anything else?"

"We get a fruit basket from the Joint Chiefs of Staff every Christmas --"

"In other words, you don't know anything."

"What are you getting at?"

"Just this: Budd Dugan was never in the Navy."

"Well, I knew that --"

"He _worked_ for the Navy, Chuck, but he was never _in_ the Navy, because then he would've had to follow Naval Law."

"While he did what?"

"Hunted down traitors and spies."

Chuck closed his good eye. Sally watched him. They were both starting to shiver. The water was freezing.

"Hard job," Chuck finally said.

"Dangerous," Sally agreed.

"But I don't see --"

"There's an ongoing investigation, Chuck. Corruption of a Senior Officer. Treason. Murder. Espionage. And this Battle Plan here is the final piece of the puzzle."

"Conclusions?" Chuck whispered.

She gave it to him straight. "The Admiral killed your dad."

The line attached to her wrist jumped.

T U G   T U G   T U G T U G T U G T U G T U G T U G

"What did that mean?"

"I don't know." Sally gave two tugs back.

REPEAT MESSAGE.

"Come on, Chuck," she said, "there's nothing down here for us left to --!" Sally was yanked into the water and dragged out the Stateroom door.

Chuck was left holding her diving mask.

He fitted his own in place, bit his mouthpiece, and dove into the water, kicking hard. He found Sally at the end of the maindeck hall, wedged behind a hatch, one arm outside, still connected to the nylon twine. She was fighting to free herself, banging against the door frame.

Chuck swam up, removed his trusty buck-knife

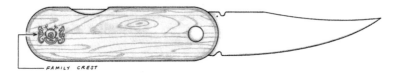

FAMILY CREST

and cut the line. They fell back into the hall. Her eyes were shut tight. She was holding her breath. The loose mouthpiece was sending bubbles everywhere. Chuck stuck it back between her teeth and pressed the mask over her eyes. She continued to panic and struggle with him. Chuck spit out his own air supply and brought his face close to her ear.

In his deepest underwater bellow, he shouted the bubbly words:

CALM DOWN
AND BREATHE!

By the time they reached the surface, eight
minutes later, the water had turned a steamship gray
and was full of seaweed and silt. The waves lurched
chaotically. They could see it from under water: a
storm had hit.

A summer squall, nearing its full violence.
Fifteen-foot seas. It took them several minutes of
shouting, waving, and turning in place before they
spotted the _Fiddle_-_Dee_-_Dee_, laboring at two-thirds
engine speed just trying to stay in position.

As Chuck and Sally swam over, a colossal wave
plucked them up and brought them crashing onto the
boat. Chuck put his knee through a window. Sally was
bleeding from the wrist.

"ARE YOU ALL RIGHT, SIR?" Brace hollered.

"YES. CHECK ON SALLY." Chuck went inside and
found his mother at the wheel, struggling to keep the
boat's nose into the wind.

"Out of the clear blue," she muttered through
gritted teeth. "Maybe sixty seconds warning. I think
we'll be all right if we can outrun these high seas.
Trouble is, we're shipping an awful lot of water.
If the engine floods, we might as well abandon --"

"Isn't the pump working?" Chuck asked. He
stripped off his wet suit to bandage his bleeding knee.

Fraunces leaned over a dial on the dash. She
cupped her hands to read it. They had a motorized
bilge pump that went on automatically. "No, it isn't."

"I'll take a look at it."

"Tie yourself down!" she shouted as the door
opened and Brace and Sally entered, the downpour
slipping inside with them.

"I'll be all right!" Chuck yelled.

He stepped past the butler, out the door -- <u>the
wind</u> <u>was</u> <u>unearthly</u>! -- and closed it behind him. He
inched forward, gripping the rail with both hands.

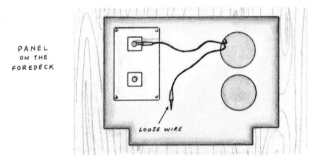

PANEL
ON THE
FOREDECK

LOOSE WIRE

Chuck fought to keep himself in one place as he
removed the cowling and re-connected the reserve
battery to the pump. He saw it spark, saw that power

had been restored, and re-sealed the cover tight.

He turned back to the cabin, expecting to see his mother give him either a thumbs-up or a thumbs-down.

Fraunces, Brace, and Sally were waving their arms. Why were they doing that?

He was about to shout the words, "What does that mean?" when he realized, _of course_, what that meant. Turning, knowing what was coming, he faced the mountain of water as it towered over him --

At least the pump is working, Chuck thought as he shot into space.

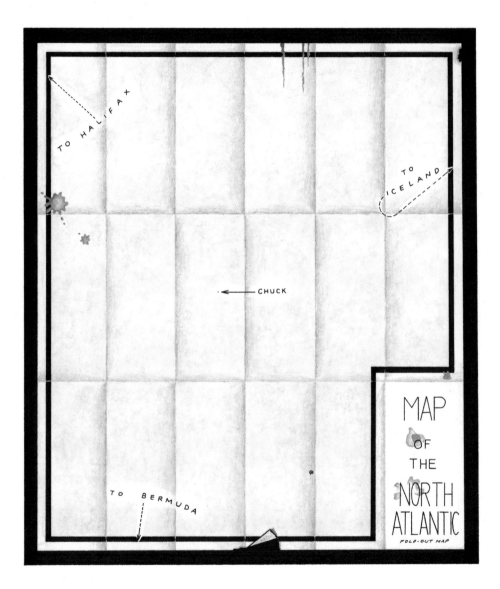

*** Chapter Twelve ***
TREADING WATER

He spent the first hour just surviving the storm. Endlessly scrambling to the tops of waves only to sink back into the troughs. Battered and soaked, dizzy -- and <u>very</u> <u>tired</u>.

Another hour spent turning in circles, yelling for the boat.

He was utterly alone.

With the freak summertime squall over, the sun had returned, the overcast skies banished. It was getting hot. As the air warmed, the sea became more co-operative. By two o'clock, the weather was beautiful. From the wave crests, Chuck estimated he had fifteen miles of unimpaired visibility. He saw blue sky in every direction. And nothing else.

He could feel the current: strong, whisking him into the North Atlantic. No way to get off, and no-where to swim to. He was caught in the Gulf Stream.

Next stop ... Iceland, Chuck thought. I've always wanted to visit.

He was a resilient person, not given over to negativity. But at a certain point, sooner or later, he was going to either:

a) freeze to death, or

b) drown.

Whichever came first.

By the time he'd been treading water for four hours, he realized he needed to make some hard choices. He'd never timed himself before, and he hesitated to imagine what his limits might be. It was a scary thought. But he squared himself to the situation -- it was unavoidable -- and put a conservative number on it: eight hours.

Yes. He could definitely last that long.

Probably not ten.

His only moment of excitement had been the <u>fin</u>,

around five o'clock.

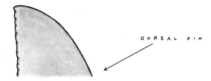

Thank God I patched up that bloody knee, he thought. A shark alone he could handle -- even if it attacked him. A <u>family</u> of sharks, a <u>frenzy</u> -- with Chuck's knee the shark appetizer -- that he could do without.

There was a hopeful moment at sunset.

OFF-SHORE
DRILLING RIG

TOO FAR AWAY

He waved and screamed himself hoarse, but the drilling platform was ten miles away if it was an inch, and he was one red head in a vast blue ocean. If that's what I can expect in the way of HOPE, he thought, maybe I'd be better off WITHOUT it.

He quit that line of thinking immediately.

The Admiral -- Chuck's eye took on a dark gleam when thinking of the man -- if I could just get my hands on him.

He put the question to himself: Could I kill him?

He wasn't sure. He'd never killed anyone before, and he hoped he never would. But he really thought -- yes, he could kill that man.

It was the ADMIRAL, he thought grimly. Down through the years. All this time ...

He tried to picture it. "The murder of your father." But he couldn't get a fix. The steps leading up to such an act of pure evil were not clear to him.

If the Admiral was the skipper of the Minuteman, he must have known Budd. That was even harder for Chuck to imagine. Later on, the Admiral must have gotten wind that Budd was on to him -- but then what?

And what happened onboard the Minuteman?

Yankee torpedo? German sailors?

He gave a shout of frustration. What a position to be in! Treading water with a headful of unanswered questions. He realized that, yes, he'd never been trained for intelligence work, but it was more than that. He wasn't built for it. The conclusions -- and the suspicions that generated them -- hung separate and unconnectable in Chuck's mind. He wanted to give it meaning. To make sense of it all.

But maybe it'll never make sense, he thought.

Maybe that's the thing with a Bad Guy, a Crook, a Desperado: you'll never get it to add up to something satisfactory. Not if you live to be a hundred or get decorated for valor in action.

THE NAVY CROSS
FOR HEROISM

That was something he understood, all right.

ACTION.

What line of the Service will I go into? Chuck wondered dreamily, for the thousandth time, a faint smile appearing on his sunburnt face. Something that would make Budd proud. Something tricky -- underwater demolition, say. Or else --

His stomach fell. He was AWOL. There was not going to be any career in the Service. No more Naval Academy. No more Navy. He was going to jail. Or Canada.

He felt miserable. The cold waves closed over his head, and he sank from view. But when he bobbed to the surface a moment later, a fresh glint was in his eye.

He was thinking about VICTORY.

It hadn't occurred to him before -- there hadn't been time -- but they'd <u>won</u> last night. "The Battle for Chertsey Island." He'd <u>done</u> it: he'd gotten rid of the Admiral and his boys. Almost single-handedly. And at not <u>too</u> great a personal cost. A smashed POPCYCLE, a busted head, a few broken toes, his naval career down the drain.

And his inheritance. Whatever that was.

Suddenly hungry -- and sick to death of treading water, endlessly cycling in one place -- he dove deep into the ocean. By a lucky chance, he hadn't dumped his diving mask with his air tanks and wet suit. It had been around his neck when he was swept over and had protected him from the lashing rain of the storm. Now, he put it back on and went fishing.

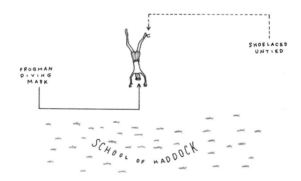

On his third dive, he spotted a thick school of haddock. He drifted as close as possible, letting out just enough air to hang suspended, upside-down, then went dead in the water. The school shifted direction, and suddenly they were all around him ... everywhere ... twinkling in the light ... miraculous ... never touching him.

He flexed his hand.

The school vanished in a blaze of silver.

But he came out of the water, gripping for all he was worth, one healthy fish.

He slipped his mask down and examined his catch.

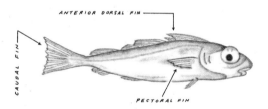

It was probably safer <u>not</u> to eat it, because digestion would make him tired. But he was going to get dehydrated sooner or later, and a fish was the only way he could think of to get fresh liquid back in his system.

So he swallowed it. Alive. One whole fish. It

was hard to do, but he got it down all right, felt it wriggling in his stomach.

The thing you miss most at a time like this, Chuck told himself, is having a pair of diving fins.

He thought about that for a moment. Oh yes. Diving fins. Obviously. He gave a huge yawn.

No -- the thing you miss most at a time like this is having a submarine bike. Now that would be the perfect thing to have.

Feeling sleepy, he closed his eye and grinned, remembering with pride the maiden voyage of his submarine bike. He'd been keeping her under wraps. "The POPCYCLE." He gave a chuckle. It would go down in family legend, that night. A Launch unlike other launches, a Victory unlike other victories, an Adventure unlike other ...

He woke in a panic some time later. He had no idea where he was. The sun had set. It was night. Something jogged his elbow in the dark.

"I'm here!" he cried. "Hello? Mom? Sally?"

He heard loud swooshing noises, felt things, large things, passing all around him in the darkness. Terrified, he remembered where he was.

He'd been treading water in his sleep! A pod of whales had woken him.

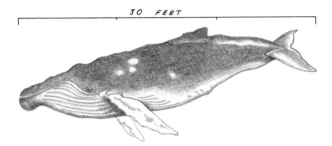

30 FEET

Huge, slow-moving humpbacks. What seemed like dozens. As they moved past, several nudged him. After the initial fear and disorientation had passed, Chuck burst out laughing. "Hello, whales!" He reached out and patted their thick blubber. "Thanks for the wake-up call!"

A geyser of spray showered down on him. A wild thought: hitch a ride!

But before he could grab a fin long enough to haul himself onboard -- or find out whether this was a physical possibility -- the whales began their feeding dive, disappearing in twos and threes. Within another thirty seconds, they were all gone.

Chuck stretched, yawned. <u>There</u>! -- he felt the

cramp. Ominous. The twinge that signaled the beginning of the end.

"Backfloat," he said. He kicked and leaned back, spreading his arms and legs wide in the water, trying to relax the stitch in his side. He contemplated the fat yellow moon staring him in the face.

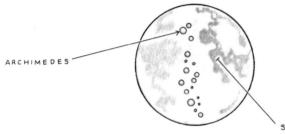

ARCHIMEDES

SEA OF TRANQUILITY

An hour passed. His breathing was shallow. It was very peaceful out here.

Another hour. He wondered how long he'd been at it. At least ten hours.

He dozed intermittently. He could no longer feel his legs. His teeth had stopped chattering; he didn't know what that meant, assumed it was a bad sign.

Another hour.

Chuck lay balanced flat on the surface. He dipped below as he exhaled, inhaling a tiny gulp at the final moment, and it was just enough to bring him slowly back to sea level again, the air in his lungs the only thing left keeping him afloat. He routinely forgot where he was. Is this Dahlgren Hall? he wondered. Who turned out the lights?

He passed under a wave and came up reciting the Midshipman's Table of Priorities.

"Midshipmen --" he began, his voice cracked and faint. He spat out some water. "-- will use the Table of Priorities when determining the precedence of one activity over another. ONE. Orders to report to the Superintendent, Commandant, Deputy Commandant."

He went under. Slowly, he returned.

"TWO. Emergency calls for immediate medical and dental care. THREE ..."

He disappeared.

"ELEVEN. Appointment with academic advisor during pre-registration each semester ... TWENTY-FOUR. Liberty."

Now his whales were back, jostling and sliding all around him in the blackness. This time he could not reach out to touch them.

"Thanks, boys, but I'm done for. Tell 'em good-bye for me. I'll be seeing you."

He exhaled, began to sink, quickly inhaled --
disappeared -- and reappeared for the final time.

"I, Chuck Dugan," he said softly, "having been
appointed a Midshipman in the United States Navy, do
solemnly swear that I will support and defend the
Constitution of the United States against all enemies,
foreign and domestic --"

He was gone.

A freshening breeze rippled the water. The moon
continued to shine. It seemed strange that he had ever
been in such a lonely place.

A few bubbles popped. All the air left in a young
man's lungs.

Then a few more bubbles. Maybe a passing sea
bass.

Then millions of bubbles, torrents of bubbles,
bursting and cascading, jets of water sallying into
the air. In the midst of this, the gray submarine
turret broke through the surface, followed by the long
iron deck halved by a narrow wooden catwalk, and
flanked by hissing gunmetal. Water streaming off,
motors whirring, flags whipping in the night air.

Chuck lay motionless on the U-boat's deck. Was

he dead? No: Chuck Dugan would not drown that easily.
An air bubble formed on his lips and broke. He made
the sound: "Ah-ha."

He inhaled and gave a wet cough. He could not
move his body, but he could hear the sound of men
behind him: boot steps climbing down the wing and
clamping forward up the ship.

He felt the sudden brightness and heat of a
spotlight being aimed at him. His good eye opened a
crack. He saw the pennant flying overhead

and he fell back, into nothingness.

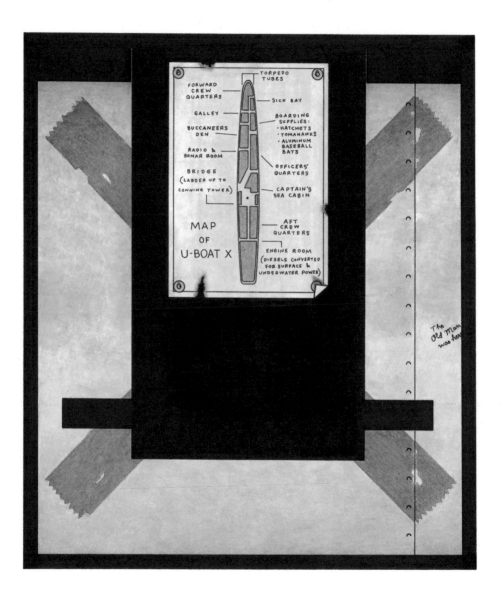

*** Chapter Thirteen ***

WITH THE BUCCANEERS OF U-BOAT X

"Wake up, mac," the voice said, slapping Chuck's face.

Blindfolded, Chuck had no memory of where he was. But an instinct told him not to cry out, not to move. He could hear the heavy throb of diesels inside a closed iron space, the slosh of water passing overhead.

Submarine sounds.

With an effort, he tried to identify the engines by their pitch.

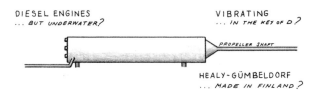

DIESEL ENGINES
... *BUT UNDERWATER?*

VIBRATING
... *IN THE KEY OF D?*

PROPELLER SHAFT

HEALY-GÜMBELDORF
... *MADE IN FINLAND?*

And -- did one have a warped axle?

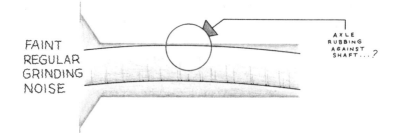

FAINT REGULAR GRINDING NOISE

AXLE RUBBING AGAINST SHAFT...?

Impossible to say without looking.

Then a noise inside the room with him -- what was THAT? -- metal rasping softly against metal. A knife.

I'm a dead man, Chuck thought.

The blade touched his bare wrist. Chuck flinched. Then his bonds parted, the ropes that had been tying his hands together separated. His blindfold was ripped away. And Chuck felt himself swaying freely in the air: a hammock. He must have spent the night in it. He kept his eyes shut tight against the sudden brightness.

"Hot coffee, mac," the voice said. "Take it or leave it."

Chuck tried to consider the situation carefully, but his thoughts were muddled. He didn't want to co-operate if he was a POW. There were rules to that: strict Geneva Convention. Don't co-operate, don't

give out more than your Name, Rank, and Serial Number.
Since this was his first experience as a captive --
which he assumed he was, though he couldn't remember
whose or which war -- he wanted to get it right.

Then he heard another voice. Shouting in the
distance. Giving orders. The sound came muffled,
through several bulkheads, from another part of the
ship. The message was lost, but the words were unmistakable: German.

Two unwelcome memories of the night before
floated into Chuck's mind:

First, the submarine was a U-boat. Of all things.
A German U-boat! There was no question about that.

Second, he had seen the Black Flag. The "Jolly
Roger," the standard that bore the words:

ABANDON ALL HOPE...
CUT YOUR ENGINES AND HEAVE-TO
OR WE KILL EVERY LIVING SOUL.
...WE GIVE NO QUARTER.
DO OR DIE.

Chuck gave a convulsive shiver.

"Mac," the voice said, "open your eyes and take

this cup of coffee or else."

Chuck opened his good eye. He took the cup of
coffee. "Thanks," he said.

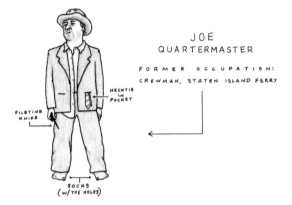

The sailor called Joe nodded. "Don't mention
it, mac." Then he leaned back against the bulkhead
and picked his teeth with the gleaming silver tip of
his knife.

Chuck sat quietly for a moment. He took a sip of
the coffee -- Navy-style black and boiling hot. For
an instant, he felt faint, his head reeling from the
on-rush of heat.

"Steady as she goes, mac."

Blood pumping loud in his ears, Chuck gripped
the mug tight. After a moment, his head cleared, and
he was left feeling -- how would he put it -- <u>oddly</u>

comforted. He wondered stupidly at this sensation for a moment, then realized part of it had to do with the shape of the mug itself. He looked down, turning it in his hands.

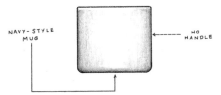

He shook his head, squinting. Navy mugs were indeed familiar to him. But it was more than that. There was something else going on here. What was it?

At first, he was only dimly aware of the ringing bell. Clear, twice-struck, eight-times-repeated. Eight bells. He counted them instinctively. Start the forenoon watch: breakfast is over.

"Hey," Chuck cried. "A ship's clock."

He was on a ship with some standards of Navy life, and the thought encouraged him enormously.

"Sir?" he said, looking up at the sailor called Joe. "Where am I?"

"U-boat X."

Chuck frowned. This meant nothing to him. He asked the question again.

"X, mac, X," the sailor repeated. "Well," he said, straightening, "I did what I came for. Nose around the bucket if you want. Nobody's gonna mess with you. Probably." He turned to leave.

"Excuse me, sir --"

"Sir?" Outraged by Chuck's courtesy. "I look like an officer to you, mac?"

Chuck was silent.

"What should I call you?"

"On this bucket, we say mate, mac. Now what's your question?"

"Am I your prisoner or not?"

Joe shrugged. "Who knows, mac, I sure don't. Play your cards right, you may come out of this with a job." He walked out the doorway.

Chuck eased himself upright in the hammock, balancing the mug with care, and sipped his coffee. He was feeling pretty good, all things considered. He'd slept well: he could feel it, although his muscles had never been so stiff. He was lucky to be alive. But he was also extremely hungry. He longed -- briefly but intensely -- for a tuna-fish sandwich and a cold glass of milk. Then decided coffee was very much all right.

Mainly, he felt curious.

U-boat X ... he mused. I wonder if it's the same ship, the same U-boat that ... he paused uncertainly ... that what? Sank the _Minuteman_? That's not possible. You saw it yourself: an American torpedo. Although, he countered, there were U-boat sailors aboard when she went down -- you saw that too.

He shook his head. Still a puzzle.

He slid from the hammock onto the deck, testing his legs. So good so far. He set the empty mug on the counter and followed the way Joe had gone.

"What did you mean by a _job_?" he asked, once he'd caught up. They were moving aft, down the cramped passageway. The ambient light was dim, battle-ready blue, punctuated by glowing strips of amber-yellow.

Joe answered over his shoulder.

"The Old Man's _always_ looking for fresh buckos, mac."

Two sailors, squeezing past, raised their hands in greeting. "Morning, mate," they said.

"Morning, mates," Joe answered.

Seeing Chuck, one sailor lunged forward, a straight razor in his hand, and pinned Chuck to the wall. The other pulled a machete from his waistband and raised it over his head like he was about to chop Chuck in half.

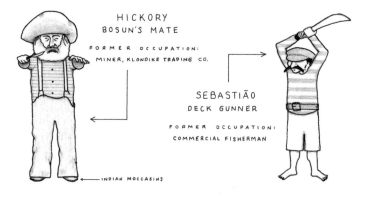

HICKORY
BOSUN'S MATE
FORMER OCCUPATION:
MINER, KLONDIKE TRADING CO.

SEBASTIÃO
DECK GUNNER
FORMER OCCUPATION:
COMMERCIAL FISHERMAN

INDIAN MOCCASINS

Joe, observing mechanically, said, "Fresh bucko here, mates," turned, and walked away.

The sailors stared at Chuck for a moment. "Morning, mate," they said and continued up the ship as if nothing had happened.

Chuck gave an uneasy cough and shook his head. He passed through the crowded Control Room without anyone taking further notice of him.

"The Old Man," he said, catching up with Joe. "Is that the Captain of this vessel?"

"You think we got a President onboard, mac?"

"Aren't you guys supposed to be Germans or something?"

"Brooklyn, mac -- what do I sound like? There's two Germans right now. But only one of them is from the old days."

Chuck thought about this. "From the War, you mean."

Joe nodded. "The First Officer."

"But you're not from the old days."

"Mac, I'm an American."

Chuck nodded haggardly. "I'm AWOL."

Joe gave a grunt. "Don't be ashamed of it, mac. I'm AWOL from the Cops, the Mob, and the Staten Island Ferry -- take yer pick."

"What?"

Joe nodded. "Every bucko on this ship's running from somebody or other. INTERPOL, Soviet Army, IRS, nagging wives ..."

Chuck asked: "Who are you people?"

Joe spread his arms, touching either side of the

cramped corridor, and announced:

"We're the Buccaneers of U-boat X, mac. We prowl
the seven seas and take no prisoners. Everyone and
everything is fair game, and the only rule is: Look out
for your mates. Actually, we used to be a pretty rowdy
crew, but when the Old Man took over a few years back,
we had to shape up or ship out. The Old Man runs a
taut U-boat, mac. Give him any grief? You walk the
plank. Cut up on duty? You walk the plank. And don't
think he'll cut you any slack just because he has --"
Joe lowered his voice "-- A-M-N-E-S-I-A, mac. What
ails the Old Man is strictly long-term. So mind your Ps
and Qs. Anything you pull aboard this vessel, you'll --"

"Walk the plank. I get it."

"I was gonna say 'be keel-hauled for.' We do
that, too. Take the Engineer here --"

They had reached the Engine Room by now.

"Morning, mate," the Engineer said.

"Morning, mate," Joe replied. He pointed at the
Engineer. "He jumped ship from the Japanese Navy."

The Engineer smiled proudly.

The faint, regular grinding noise Chuck had
heard earlier was much more pronounced.

Chuck spoke sharply: "Engineer, you've got a bent axle -- can't you hear it? It's wearing on the inside of the shaft."

The Engineer's smile faded, and he cast a quizzical look at Joe, who shrugged. "Mac here is some kind of fugitive junior officer. Or else he's nuts."

The Engineer turned back to Chuck and shrugged. "It was always like this."

"No, it wasn't." Chuck took a step forward.

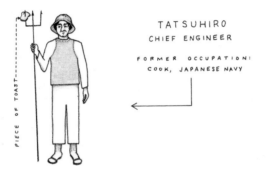

PIECE OF TOAST

TATSUHIRO
CHIEF ENGINEER

FORMER OCCUPATION:
COOK, JAPANESE NAVY

The Engineer snatched up a long, sharpened trident spear that was normally used to make toast and aimed it fiercely at Chuck's head. Brushing the tips aside, Chuck made his way past the Engineer to the engines, pressing his ear to each of them in turn, like a doctor listening to his patient's breathing. Then he stepped back.

"<u>This</u> one," he said. "Port Screw, Number Two. Shut it down, and we'll hammer out the trouble in half a bell."

Gripping the spear, the Engineer stared blankly at Chuck and made no reply. Something in the man's stubbornness gave Chuck pause. "You can run on one engine, you know."

The Engineer shook his head. "Impossible."

"It's easy," Chuck said. "Watch."

"What are you <u>doing</u>?" the Engineer groaned.

A few minutes later, the brass communicating tube on the wall gave a whistle. Chuck spoke into it.

"Engine Room," he announced. "Midshipman Third Class Dugan here."

"This is the Captain. Why have we slowed to half-speed?"

"Sir, chronic trouble detected in the port shaft. Commenced running under starboard power. Estimate fifteen minutes of repair time, sir, and we should be able to squeeze another four knots out of her."

There was a pause on the other end. "Carry on."

"Aye-aye, sir. OK, mates ..." Chuck spit into his palms.

Twenty minutes later, operating at full power, Chuck, Joe, and the Engineer were eating toast and drinking coffee when alarms broke out all over the ship. The change was sudden, instantly transforming the tranquil morning that had preceded it into a tense, worried scramble.

"What's happening!" Chuck asked as they hustled forward up the ship.

"General Quarters," Joe answered. "Battle Stations."

"What's yours?"

"Torpedo Command."

"On the bridge?"

"Right."

"Mind if I tag along?"

"Long as you keep quiet, mac."

They arrived at the Control Room. Compared to other ships, it was tiny. Aware of the space limitations, Chuck made himself as small as he could, pressed against the wall, watching with wide eyes. For him, it was the first time when going to "Battle Stations" had not been a drill.

"This the new man, Joe?" a voice asked.

"Yessir."

"What's he doing up here?"

"He knows his stuff, sir. He just fixed Engine No. 2."

"The one that makes the grinding noise?"

"Yessir."

A tall man whose bearded face was a mass of scars stepped into the light and gave Chuck a silent once-over.

THE OLD MAN
CAPTAIN

FORMER OCCUPATION:
UNKNOWN

KILLER WHALE BONE CANE

"Identify the contact," he said.

"U.S. Navy patrol vessel, Captain."

"Bearing and position?"

"A thousand yards, sir. Dead ahead. Moving south, same as us."

Chuck frowned to himself. Patrol vessel?

"She hear us?" the Old Man asked.

"I don't think so, sir: no change in bearing."

"Steady as she goes."

Chuck felt a stab of alarm. He needed to say something. It was urgent. Despite Joe's warning, he couldn't keep quiet:

"Permission to observe through the periscope, sir!"

All eyes turned on Chuck. The quick, tense working of the ship stopped. Joe, responsible for bringing him here, winced and looked at his feet.

"Granted," the Old Man said.

Chuck moved solemnly to the periscope and looked at the surface image.

There he is, Chuck thought. I knew it.

"She's the USS <u>Kestrel</u>, sir," he reported. "<u>Mohawk</u>-class patrol boat. Two deck-mounted .50-caliber machine-guns, fore and aft. Six torpedoes. And a pair of Ajax sea mines."

Chuck stepped away, relinquishing the periscope.

"Thank you, sailor," the Old Man said, sounding

impressed. "Men," he announced, "sounds like we better
steer clear of this one --"

"Captain, I'm sorry to interrupt, but I've got
something else to tell you about this ship."

The Captain stared expectantly at Chuck. "Let's
hear it."

"Yessir. She's skippered by a <u>traitor</u>, sir --
an enemy of the United States. Spy, murderer, war
criminal. Known as 'The Admiral.' There's a good
chance that --" Chuck broke off, suddenly lost in
thought.

Was he sure about this? Was <u>this</u> the way? What
about the System? The Naval Codes of Justice? What
about the Rules he'd been studying and training for,
that he believed in with every fiber of his being? <u>What
would <u>Sally</u> say</u>? His thoughts raced past in a blur of
conflicting questions and unspoken doubts.

The Old Man was waiting.

Chuck gave a sigh. He was on his own. "Captain,"
he finally said. "The Navy wouldn't shed any tears, if
you get me. Not only that, but his crew is composed
entirely of three miscreant <u>boys</u> -- sons of his. I

can't feature them firing even once before you got off a barrage big enough to send the whole damn ship to Davy Jones's locker!"

In a heavy German accent, the First Officer broke the uneasy silence that followed. "Just a moment, Captain." He stepped into the light, and Chuck got his first good look at the only crew member from "the old days" of the War.

NUMBER ONE

FIRST OFFICER

FORMER OCCUPATION:
SAME

"You say she's the <u>Kestrel</u>?" he asked.

A look of surprise on Chuck's face.

"Yessir."

"The Admiral's boat?"

"You know him, sir?"

"Captain," the First Officer said. "I have information to report, too."

"Let's have it, by God."

"This is the man who murdered the crew back in

'42 and condemned us to a life of piracy." He peered
into the periscope and cursed in German. Then he
straightened. "The swine who double-crossed our
former captain and sent twenty-nine of thirty-eight
sailors to hell in a crooked arms deal gone awry on
a moonless night in April of 1942."

"Sink the bastard."

"Aye-aye, Captain."

Shouted commands, ringing bells for action --
the hydraulic whoosh of outgoing torpedoes -- and
the crew waited eagerly for the spoils of the day.

Chuck's mind, apart from wondering where the
Buccaneers of U-boat X got their spare torpedoes
from, was curiously blank.

B - O - O - O - M.

The rumble of distant explosions reached them.

"She's on fire," the First Officer reported.
"Sinking fast."

It was not until the cheering broke out that
Chuck remembered his inheritance -- the Treasure --
aboard the targeted vessel. He considered asking the
navigator for a precise fix of their current
whereabouts -- if he'd found one wreck, he could always

find another -- but then he stopped himself. Perhaps this paid for the sin he had just committed. The sin of condemning those three boys to their deaths. After all: even if they weren't innocent, they were only boys.

"Son?" The Old Man said.

Chuck was lost in thought. He looked up. "Yessir?"

"Tell me something. Could you use a job?"

From across the Control Room, Joe gave Chuck a nod and said: "Welcome aboard, mate."

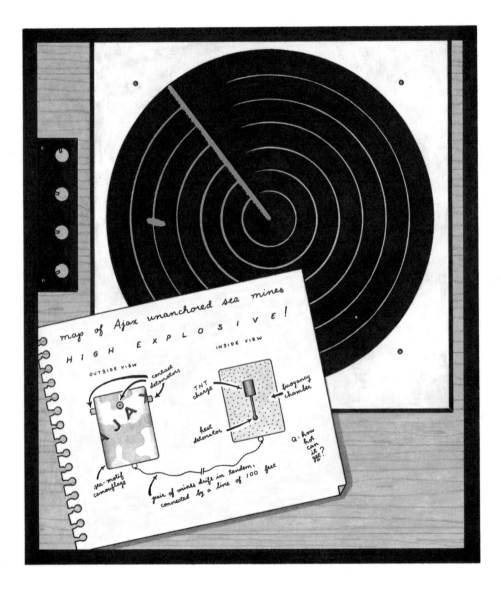

*** Chapter Fourteen ***

LOSS OF LIFE

The instant Chuck had been swept overboard,
Sally ran on deck and threw out a lifeboat. She yanked
the ripcord and watched the bright orange raft
disappear into the storm.

Afterward, praying Chuck had made it safely
aboard, Sally, Fraunces, and Brace focused their
efforts on finding the lifeboat again

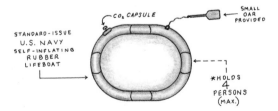

STANDARD-ISSUE
U.S. NAVY
SELF-INFLATING
RUBBER
LIFEBOAT

CO₂ CAPSULE

SMALL
OAR
PROVIDED

*HOLDS
4
PERSONS
(MAX.)

since it would show on radar. Whereas Chuck, alone on the ocean, would not.

The Coast Guard refused to help. Chuck Dugan had been reported "Lost At Sea" three times in the past three days, and the crew of the Fiddle-Dee-Dee was now wanted for criminal mischief. "You're on your own," the Coast Guard said.

On their own. Through the night, with a vigilant eye on the radar scope, they sailed deep into the Atlantic.

"He'll be all right," Sally said at regular intervals. "Chuck holds five long-distance swimming records, you know. He found the lifeboat ... and we'll find him."

Brace nodded thoughtfully, handing her a cup of coffee. "Provided," he said, "we don't run out of fuel first."

Dawn brought a glimmer of hope: a strong signal from the south. Another vessel. She might have seen something, heard something -- rescued Chuck. No response to their radio calls, they cranked the wheel, gunned the engines, and headed straight for her.

All that remained of the mysterious vessel, by the time they caught up, was a cloud of smoke.

"What <u>happened</u>?" Fraunces asked.

<u>Explosion</u>, Sally noted. She identified the scent on the air: <u>Cordite</u>.

The sea was littered with wreckage and ash.

"Madam ...?"

"Yes, Brace?"

The butler was squinting into the distance. He pointed. "What do you make of the curious bulbous objects floating away to starboard?"

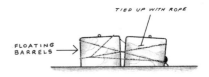

"They appear to be barrels."

"Indeed, madam. But isn't that a person attached?"

"I doubt it."

"The barrels, ahoy!" Brace waved his arm. "Person at the barrels! Your attention, if you please!"

A limp, bedraggled hand reached up from the water and waved back.

"Good Lord!" Fraunces gasped.

They brought the boat around. Here is what they found:

"I surrender," Misha said.

Inexplicably lashed to the barrels -- which were not "barrels," of course, but a pair of Ajax sea mines being used as rescue floats -- Misha had to be hauled aboard and separated from them on the bridge.

In response to their questions, Misha glared fixedly into space until finally he seemed to erupt: "The son of a bitch cheated me! They were all short!"

Then he folded his arms over his chest and refused to say another word.

Brace and Sally took him below and locked Misha in one of the forward berths. When they returned, Fraunces yelled for them to come to the bridge.

She pointed at the top of the radar screen.

"Look at this," she said.

After a brief discussion, they agreed to use up whatever remained in the fuel tanks -- an hour's worth at most -- to track the unknown signal.

"We'll just keep going," Fraunces said, her voice tight with exhaustion. None of them had slept. "We'll see where it leads."

It led to an island.

Entering the lagoon, on the south side, they found scraggly palm trees bordering a sandy beach.

"There!" Sally said, pointing.

Pulled up clear of the water lay a bright orange lifeboat made of rubber, now deflated, used up.

"Clever lad," said Brace. He closed his eyes, put his hand to his heart, and heaved a sigh of relief. "He <u>did it</u>."

They ran the <u>Fiddle</u>-<u>Dee</u>-<u>Dee</u> aground on the shallows and waded ashore.

"Footprints!" Fraunces cried.

The trail led up the beach and into the trees. Fraunces and Brace followed, calling out Chuck's name. They soon disappeared from view.

Sally, Specimen Case in hand, remained on the beach. Something was wrong: the footprints belonged to more than one person. Stooping, she examined the tracks more closely. One stuck out.

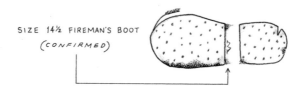

SIZE 14½ FIREMAN'S BOOT
(CONFIRMED)

"Uh-oh."

She lifted the lifeboat and found letters stamped
on the rubber underneath -- the home ship moniker --
identifying where it had come from, and who the raft
really belonged to.

It was the Admiral's lifeboat.

She named the footprints in the sand:

Harry. Stretch. The Admiral ... and Chuck? Sally
thought, the truth hitting home at last, Chuck drowned
in the storm last night. Just like anybody else would.
He never found the lifeboat you threw out.

She rose heavily to her feet, dropping the raft
on the sand. The Admiral is somewhere on this island.
And we need to leave. Now.

Under normal circumstances, she would have wept
for her friend. But there wasn't time. She entered
the water and splashed her way to the boat. She climbed
aboard and moved into the wheel house.

She knew it was her duty to arrest the Admiral. After all, that was part of her job. But she was not stupid: she needed a tactical advantage. At the moment, she didn't have one.

He must have left Misha behind for some reason.

She turned the ignition keys. The motor coughed to life. She straightened the wheel. Rudder amidships. Engines in reverse. Increase throttle steadily --

CRUNCH!

She was stuck on the sand. She revved the engines higher. Nothing. Higher still. The water around the boat churning, foaming.

The deck dipped -- What was THAT? -- as if someone had just climbed aboard the boat.

No time to worry.

She rammed the throttle controls all the way down, shifting the indicator into the position marked FULL REVERSE. The engines screamed. The wooden hull groaned. The torque made her stagger.

A voice at her elbow shouted: "Sally, what the hell are you doing?"

She jumped out of her skin. "CHUCK! You're --!"

"Fine, thanks! But what's going on?" He pointed at the thruster controls. "This is _terrible_ for the engines!"

Her head swam.

"I was supposed to be out looking for water!" he continued. "But then I saw the good old _Fiddle_-_Dee_-_Dee_ here -- what's the trouble, anyway?"

She waved away the questions. "There's no time to explain!"

The keel dragged along the bottom. With an ear-splitting noise, it broke loose. The boat, now free, began accelerating -- backward -- across the lagoon.

"The others are on-shore," Sally said, reaching for the controls, powering back. "We need to pick them up and get out of here. The Admiral is --"

Another voice. Deadly. "DON'T TOUCH THAT THROTTLE, ENSIGN."

They looked up. The Admiral stood in the doorway, holding Chuck's .45 service automatic. His uniform wet, torn in many places. A wild look in his eye. His hands unsteady.

BREECH

THUMB

GRIP

ALL
SAFETIES
OFF

* STOLEN FROM
ACADEMY ARMORY

"I survived one scrap today," he warned them in a husky voice. "I'm still armed, and I can get through another. Just keep backing up till we're clear of this basin." His eyes were skittish. He kept glancing out the windows. "Either I've gone crazy," he announced in a low tone of voice, "or there's a U-boat outside."

They continued in reverse. A rocky ride. The waves pounding against the stern.

"By the way, I'm requisitioning your vessel," he told them, waggling the gun in their direction. "Jump off any time, kiddies. Now, for example."

They were passing the rocky promontory at the mouth of the lagoon, heading for the open sea.

Chuck hadn't moved. He was staring at the Admiral. "You sank the <u>Minuteman</u>," he said quietly.

The Admiral raised his head, a look of astonishment on his face. "What did you just say?"

"You heard me," Chuck answered. "Selling guns and secrets to the Germans." Now Chuck could picture the events of that moonless night in '42. "They came aboard to make the trade. You took their dirty money. Then snuck aboard the <u>Kestrel</u>. She lay hidden in the fog, right? Afterward, the Navy called it 'Battle at Sea' and decorated you for valor -- which is a disgrace, because you were the commander and sole survivor, and should've been court-martialed for deserting your ship. But it was YOU. YOU fired the shot. That single, traitorous torpedo that sank an American vessel and wiped out her entire crew <u>JUST</u> <u>TO</u> <u>HIDE</u> <u>YOUR</u> <u>TRACKS</u>!"

Chuck's face was red. He didn't know what more to say. Finally, he stuck out his hand. "Gimme back my gun, damn you."

The Admiral looked tired. "No."

"It belongs at the Academy."

"Mine now." He thumbed back the hammer and raised the muzzle: he would fire.

Sally took a deep breath. <u>Here</u> <u>goes</u> <u>nothing</u> ... "Admiral," she began, ignoring the pistol aiming at her forehead, the boat speeding in reverse with no one at the controls. "By order of the Deputy Secretary,

Counter-Intelligence, Department of the Navy,
Washington, D.C., I hereby place you under arrest."

She took out her badge and flashed it.

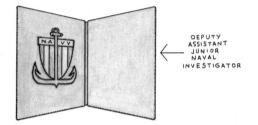

DEPUTY
ASSISTANT
JUNIOR
NAVAL
INVESTIGATOR

"The charges are High Treason, sir, and Murder
of a Federal Agent. Namely, Budd Dugan. Place the
weapon on the deck and take two steps back --"

The Admiral gave a rattling cough.

"Budd Dugan?" he spat. "_That_ sanctimonious
bastard? Don't make me laugh."

She stared back at him. "I beg your pardon?"

"Drop it," he said. "FAIR WARNING." He raised
his arm, squeezed the trigger -- BANG!

A gaping hole appeared in the wall over their
heads. Wood chips floated in the air.

"Get off now or you're both dead sailors."

Chuck's eyes were still. He was watching Misha, creeping up from the saloon deck. The flare gun from the boat's emergency kit

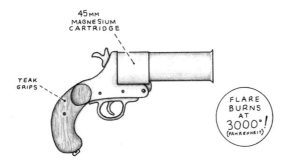

now pointed at the Admiral's back.

For the handful of seconds he remained on the bridge, Chuck finally saw the family resemblance. It was striking. Father and son. The Admiral and Misha. Same grimace, same scowl. Two men holding guns. And both about to shoot.

Any more gunplay in here, Chuck thought, is gonna start a FIRE. His heart skipped a beat. And if that happens, these two SEA MINES here will ...!

He grabbed Sally by the hand, bolted out the door, and the two of them plunged overboard.

Never a strong swimmer -- Sally had majored in medical science -- now she swam for dear life. Both of them did. Diving as fast as they could ... TEN FEET ... brains pounding ... TWENTY FEET ... hearts pumping ... THIRTY FEET ... lungs bursting to reach ... THE BOTTOM!

The water over their heads the only protection from the upcoming

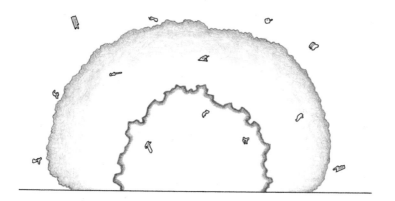

deafening explosion.

The <u>Fiddle</u>-<u>Dee</u>-<u>Dee</u> shredded herself to bits across the mouth of the lagoon. Afterward, Chuck was surprised by how many of the palm trees on-shore were left standing.

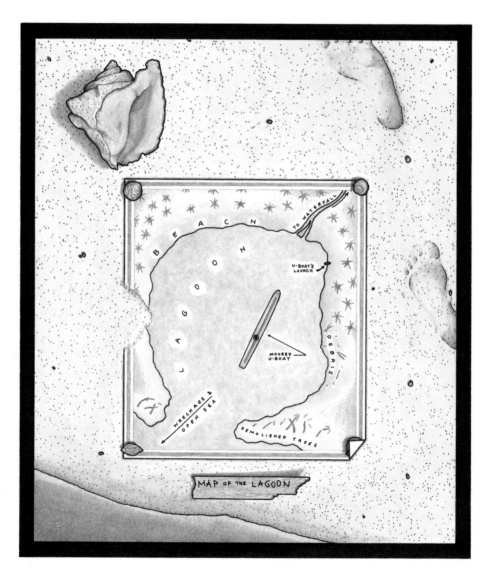

MAP OF THE LAGOON

*** **Chapter Fifteen** ***

THE SHORT STRAW

When she came across the two brothers -- Harry
and Stretch -- digging in a pool underneath a
waterfall, Fraunces realized that the lifeboat on the
beach belonged to <u>them</u>, not Chuck. She collapsed.

Then came the explosion.

Brace stuck his hand in his coat pocket and made
a gun with his index finger. "Hold it right there,
gentlemen!"

They raised their arms. "Don't shoot, Dude."

A week of guerrilla combat and a torpedo attack
on the high seas had left Harry and Stretch bruised,
shaken. They were through fighting. They helped Brace

carry Fraunces down the hill to the beach and laid
her on the sand, a conch shell clutched to her chest.

She dreamt of her son. At various ages. The
sailor -- just like his father had been.

Always growing. Every time she looked away, a new
person.

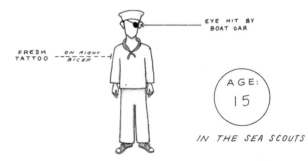

Then something happened. He didn't stop at
eighteen. He continued to grow. First he was twenty,
then thirty. Suddenly he was <u>sixty</u>, had lived a long
and prosperous life --

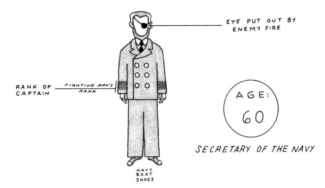

EYE PUT OUT BY
ENEMY FIRE

RANK OF
CAPTAIN

*FIGHTING MAN'S
RANK*

AGE:
60

SECRETARY OF THE NAVY

NAVY
BOAT
SHOES

-- and she knew it was only a dream. She opened her eyes.

Chuck was looking down at her. "Hi, Mom." He was
eating a papaya. "How's it going?"

She rose to her feet, fighting back a smile.

"You ... need a <u>haircut</u>, young man." She hugged
him tight. "Dear?" she asked a moment later.

"Yep?"

"Who are all these people?"

The beach was crowded. Buccaneers were filing
up and down, gathering fruit and fresh water. The
submarine's launch was ashore, being loaded with
coconuts. Preparing to return to the ship. Brace,
scavenging supplies, had traded his pocket-watch
for a tin of sardines and a pineapple.

Sally was interviewing Harry and Stretch.

"First, you were attacked," she said. She was reading from her notes. "Then, you abandoned ship. I'm with you so far. What I want to know is this: why did you leave a man behind?" She was referring to Misha.

Stretch gave a shrug. "Not enough room."

"Your lifeboat seats <u>four</u>," she said. "How many of you were there?"

"Five."

Sally frowned. "There was a fifth man? Who?"

Harry interrupted. "Four <u>people</u>, Dude," he clarified. "But Dad said we couldn't afford to leave the Treasure behind, so --"

"One of us would have to make the Ultimate Sacrifice." Stretch picked his nose philosophically.

<u>So</u> <u>that</u> <u>was</u> <u>it</u>, Sally thought. An argument over the Treasure. Ending in the loss of a son. "Then what?"

"He made us draw straws --"

"Matches, Dude."

"Loser drew the short match."

They described the setup. It seemed innocent enough. But Sally saw the ruse: all four matches in his hand, the Admiral had simply <u>squeezed</u> ...

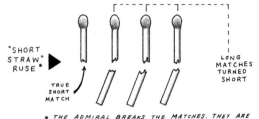

"SHORT
STRAW"
RUSE *

TRUE
SHORT
MATCH

LONG
MATCHES
TURNED
SHORT

* THE ADMIRAL BREAKS THE MATCHES. THEY ARE
NOW ALL SHORT. THE FIRST MAN WHO CHOOSES
IS THE LOSER. NO ONE ELSE CAN BE ALLOWED
TO CHOOSE OR THEY WILL SEE THE SHORT MATCHES.

Maybe the Russian planned to steal the Treasure.
Then again, Sally reflected, maybe he didn't. Maybe
his father just didn't LIKE him. She shook her head.
"Did the Admiral make Misha choose first?"

"Yeah. How did you know?"

"Lucky guess. Final question: who has the
Treasure now?"

They turned inland and gestured with mud-
spattered arms. Harry said: "He made us bury it for
safe-keeping."

"ALL ABOARD WHO'S COMING WITH US!" Joe the
Buccaneer shouted. "ALL ASHORE WHO'S <u>STAYING</u> ASHORE!
STEP LIVELY, MATES!"

"Sir?" Chuck said, leading Fraunces up to the Old
Man, standing beside the launch, smoking his pipe.

"Allow me to introduce my mother, Mrs. Dugan. Mom, this is the Captain."

"How do you do," the Old Man said.

"May I know your name, sir?"

"The Old Man."

She smiled. "I mean your proper name."

"It's the only one I've got, lady." He nodded stiffly and climbed into the boat.

"Captain ..."

He turned back. "Yes, ma'am?"

"Thank you."

"For what?"

"Saving my son's life."

He pointed at Chuck.

"That," he said, as if picking Chuck out of a crowd, "is an able-bodied sailor." He puffed on his pipe. "Anything else?"

Fraunces presented him with the conch she'd been holding. The Old Man stuck it under his arm like a hat. "Much obliged, ma'am."

Chuck reached out his hand. "Good-bye, sir."

The Old Man grasped it, and they shook. "Fair weather, son, fair weather ..."

Chuck noticed for the first time that the Old Man was missing his right thumb. But before he could examine it more closely, the Old Man released his hand, turned to the Quartermaster, and said, "These the new men, Joe?"

"Yessir."

Harry and Stretch, looking hopeful, were standing alongside the boat.

The Old Man looked them over -- Stretch managing a weak smile -- then gave a shrug and waved them aboard. "Very well. Cast off."

"Stand by the oars!"

The launch slid into the water and crossed the lagoon. The Buccaneers lashed it to the deck and boarded the sub. Bells rang out. Motors whirred. A siren's blast echoed off the rocks, and the U-boat sank from view. A trail of bubbles made its way out of the lagoon.

Sally walked down to the water, where Chuck stood in silence. "Here," she said, holding out a piece of notebook paper.

Chuck wasn't listening. He stood transfixed, staring out to sea. Had he imagined it? The familiar tattoo on the back of the Old Man's hand ...

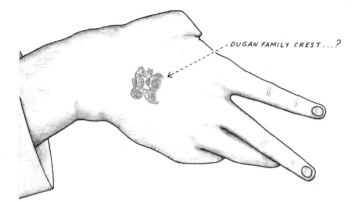

- DUGAN FAMILY CREST...?

Sally interrupted his thoughts. "You all right, Chuck?"

For a long time he didn't speak. When he did, his voice seemed faint and far away. "It's hard to say ..." he answered slowly.

"Maybe this will make you feel better." She handed him the piece of notebook paper. On it was a freshly made, updated Treasure Map.

Chuck stared at it for a moment, then folded the map up and slipped it into his pocket.

Sally was surprised. "Aren't you going up there?" she asked. "Aren't you curious?"

"I'm gonna save it ... for a rainy day."

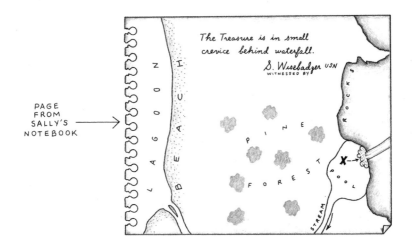

PAGE FROM SALLY'S NOTEBOOK →

The Treasure is in small crevice behind waterfall.

S. Wisebadger USN
WITNESSED BY

"Well!" Fraunces said. She and Brace joined them at the water's edge. "We appear to be marooned. <u>Now</u> what?"

Chuck turned away from the sea and faced his mother, his butler, and his company commander -- all standing in a row, watching. He gave a faint smile.

"All right," Chuck said, taking charge. "See that stack of lumber?" He aimed his thumb down the length of the beach.

A distant pile of decayed, rotten driftwood was strewn on the sand. Several ends of frayed rope were lying nearby. It looked like what it was: debris, trash from the sea.

The others turned back. "Y-es ...?"

Chuck nodded briskly.

"That's our ticket home."

It took them five hours to build the raft. Chuck drew the design in the sand with a tree limb. He'd taken an elective that spring called "Shipwrecked 101: Building from Scratch."

It being late afternoon by the time they set out, they named her the <u>Sunset</u> <u>Return</u>.

*** The End ***

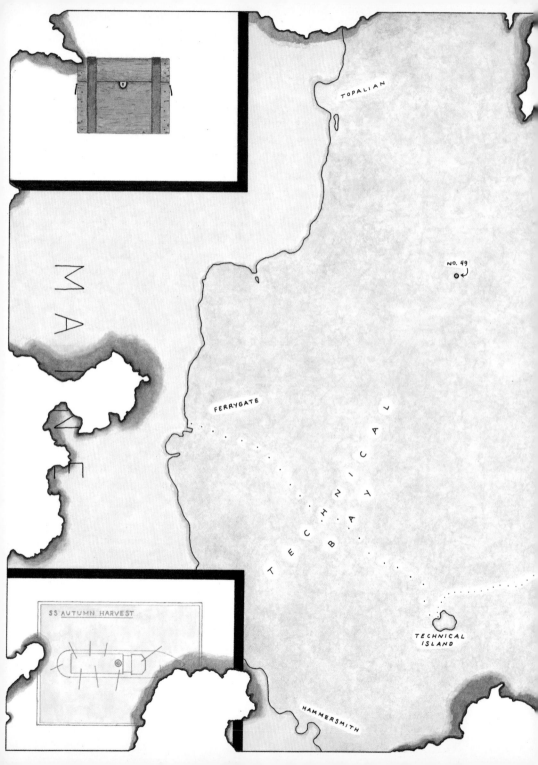

TOPALIAN

NO. 49

M A ...

FERRYGATE

T
E
C
H
N
I
C
A
L

B
A
Y

TECHNICAL
ISLAND

SS AUTUMN HARVEST

HAMMERSMITH